DOUBLE AWARD-WINNER
Bisto Book of the Year
Reading Association of Ireland Award

Norman knight and adventurer, Strongbow, has been part of Irish historical lore for centuries. But how many know the real story of his life?

Aoife is the daughter of a king who is despised by many of his peers – how will her life change after marrying Strongbow?

Morgan Llywelyn

Morgan grew up in Texas and took up writing after missing the final selection for the USA Olympic dressage team in 1975 by just half of a percentage point. Her second novel, *Lion of Ireland,* was a bestseller, and was sold around the world in twenty-seven different countries.

Morgan now lives in Ireland, and her historical fiction titles continue to sell all over the globe.

Morgan has won numerous prestigious awards, including: Best Novel of the Year (USA, National League of Penwomen); Best Novel for Young Readers (American Library Association); National Historical Society Award (USA).

Her first children's novel was *Brian Boru*, which was widely acclaimed and won a Bisto award. She has also written *Granuaile – The Pirate Queen* and *Star Dancer*.

STRONGBOW

The Story of
RICHARD AND AOIFE

MORGAN
LLYWELYN

THE O'BRIEN PRESS
DUBLIN

For Slaney and Lucia O'Brien
John Bowden
James Langan

First published 1992 by The O'Brien Press Ltd,
20 Victoria Road, Dublin 6, Ireland.
Tel: +353 1 4923333; Fax: +353 1 4922777
E-mail: books@obrien.ie
Website: www.obrien.ie
Reprinted 1993, 1994, 1998, 2000, 2002, 2004.

ISBN 0-86278-274-0

British Library Cataloguing-in-Publication Data
A catalogue record for this book is available from the British Library.

7 8 9 10 11
04 05 06 07 08

The O'Brien Press receives
assistance from

Chapter heading illustrations: Donald Teskey
Editing, layout and design: The O'Brien Press Ltd
Printing: Cox & Wyman Ltd

CONTENTS

The story is told by the two main characters –
Aoife, daughter of Dermot Mac Murrough,
and Richard de Clare, who was called Strongbow.
They give their account every second chapter.

1 *Aoife* A Wild Creature *page* 7

2 *Richard* Preparing for a Hard Life 12

3 *Aoife* An Insult to the King of Brefni 21

4 *Richard* Kings Have Ways of Getting Even 27

5 *Aoife* Urla's Wedding 35

6 *Richard* Death of a Wife 39

7 *Aoife* Fire! 45

8 *Richard* A Visitor from Ireland 49

9 *Aoife* Promises of Help 54

10 *Richard* A Kingdom of My Own 59

11 *Aoife* Terrible News 65

12 *Richard* Gathering Fighting Men 71

13 *Aoife* A King's Daughter 76

14 *Richard* Facing King Henry II 81

15 *Aoife* Normans at Baginbun 88

CONTENTS

16 *Richard* I've Come to Be a King *91*

17 *Aoife* Meeting a Future Husband *97*

18 *Richard* A Strange Irish Custom *101*

19 *Aoife* The Marriage of Aoife and Strongbow *106*

20 *Richard* A Golden Land *110*

21 *Aoife* Dermot Destroyed *116*

22 *Richard* A New King in Leinster *122*

23 *Aoife* Waiting for News *128*

24 *Richard* Siege at Dublin *130*

25 *Aoife* Holding Out *135*

26 *Richard* A Rival to Henry II *137*

27 *Aoife* The Visit of Henry *141*

28 *Richard* Tales of Aoife's Deeds *145*

29 *Aoife* Faded Hopes *150*

Epilogue Red Eva *155*

Chapter 1

AOIFE

A Wild Creature

When I was a little girl I didn't know my father was a monster. He wasn't a monster in those days, he was simply Father, a dark man with a curly beard. His beard tickled my neck when he nuzzled me, pretending to be a bear. In his growly bear-voice he'd say, 'I'm going to eat you up, Aoife. First your shoulder, then your arm, then every tender little finger. Grrr!'

This was an old game with us. 'Help, help!' I'd cry. 'Will anyone save me from this savage bear?'

Then Father would change from his bear-voice to his Father-voice that always made me feel safe and warm. 'I'll save you, Aoife,' he'd promise. 'No bear will eat you! No harm will come to you! Not while Dermot of Leinster lives.' And he'd lift me high in his arms and swing me around and around, the two of us laughing and happy together.

That was Father.

Dermot Mac Murrough, King of Leinster, must have been a different man, though they lived in the same skin. When my father rode off to do king-things I thought he was making other people happy the way he made me happy. I didn't know, in those days, that there were people who feared and hated him. I never imagined that in years to come his name would be used to frighten naughty children.

I never dreamt my father would someday be called a monster.

I didn't understand what it meant to be a king. I thought other people lived as we did, in palaces of stone with solar rooms to let in the sun so the women could sew. I thought everyone had warm clothes dyed bright colours, and arm rings of silver and copper, and gold balls to fasten their hair. Just like us.

When Father had to be away, he always came back with gifts for his families. His first family was that of his senior wife, Mor, of the clan O'Toole. She and her children had the best chambers. Mor's brother Laurence was an important priest, the Abbot of Glendalough, who would become Archbishop of Dublin one day. Father had held him hostage once, before any of us were born, and they had been friends ever since. That, I suppose, was why Father married his sister.

Father's second family was that of Sive, of the clan O'Faolain, who was my mother. Kings needed to have a lot of children, so they could have more than one wife. Father even had a son called Donal whose mother wasn't a wife of his at all. Donal Mac Murrough Kavanaugh didn't live with us, but he often came to visit us at Ferns. He was Father's oldest son, and beloved.

Father loved me most, though. Once he came back from Dublin with a Norse pony the colour of the sun, with a creamy mane and tail. It was so beautiful we all wanted it, but he gave it to me.

'This is for my merry girl, my Aoife,' Father said.

My big sister Urlacam – Urla for short – stuck out her tongue at me behind his back. But she wouldn't have ridden the pony much anyway. She had grown lazy and stayed indoors most of the time, fussing with her clothes and her hair.

I was never lazy. I'm sure that Donal and my brothers Enna and Conor never had as many adventures as I did. I went everywhere on my pony. I was awake and out under the Leinster sky almost every morning before the sun was up. I loved to gallop across the damp meadows on a summer morning, feeling the wet grass brush my bare legs. My pony loved it, too. He'd shake his thick mane and toss his head and I'd laugh out loud, I felt so good.

Once the pony threw me off and broke my arm. It hurt terribly, worse than a giant toothache. I didn't want Father to see me cry, though, so I set my jaw and tried to smile. He smiled back at me.

'My brave Aoife,' he said.

A local bone-setter took care of servants and farmers when they broke bones, but because Father was a king he had his own physician. The man was an *ollav*, the best of his profession, and he was sent for.

The ollav tugged and pulled at my arm. White lights flashed in my eyes and my ears began to ring. Father had gone off somewhere by then. No one saw me cry but the ollav and my sister Urla, who was spying on me as always.

The ollav bound my arm to a board carved with healing symbols, then wrapped it in cloths covered with a thick paste of soot and egg white and pounded comfrey root. It smelled awful.

'Your arm will heal in a moon's time,' the ollav promised, patting my cheek. His hands were very soft. 'Do you know what your name means, Aoife?' he asked.

Urla said quickly, 'It means ugly because she has such big bones, like a horse, and such bright red hair.'

The ollav frowned at my sister. 'You're wrong,' he told her. 'Aoife means radiant, beautiful.'

Father's physician had called me beautiful, and he should know. He was an educated man, not an ignorant bone-setter with rough hands! That was when I began to understand that being a king made Father special. Kings were surrounded by men like the ollav.

My arm healed. I forgot the pain. I rode my pony again and didn't let it throw me off. Father gave me a glass ball the colour of rainbows as a reward. Then he gave me a little wooden box with two leaves hinged together, each holding a tablet of wax.

'Under the law, a king's daughter may be taught to read and write,' he told me. 'You're to scribe your letters in this.' He gave me a pointed stick called a stylus and showed me how.

You see? My father was not a monster. He had become King of Leinster when he was only sixteen years old, and everyone had envied him. He had been through some hard times. But he was respected at home in Ferns, and his families loved him.

As a child, I played all the time. I played ball and chase-me and all-fall-down with my brothers and my little sister Dervla. I played with the servants' children too, and they taught me how to fish and to climb trees. My brother Enna, who was often sickly, taught me a song about a blue cow.

We ate our meals at tables of oak in the great hall. Some of the servants would smile at me when passing the food. I always smiled back. They were like part of the family, in a way. They were members of clans tributary to Father. Tributary means that their clans were not as important in Leinster as Father's clan, and so had to pay tribute to him. Sometimes that meant sending him servants for his houses. He always took very good care of these people, just as he did of us.

The servants didn't dress as well as we did, of course. To keep our feet warm in cold weather we wore *cuarans* of soft leather, with pointed toes. But servants went barefoot in all weathers.

So did I – when my mother wasn't watching. I loved to run barefoot with my long hair blowing behind me. When Mother caught me she would cluck her tongue and shake her head, and fasten my hair into horrible thick plaits that hung down my back like ropes.

But I found a way to enjoy those plaits. I loved playing rough games with the boys, because I hated to sit in the solar, sewing, like Urla. Once when my brothers and the servants' sons were playing a game of war, I picked up some long, narrow, sharp stones. I ran them through the plaits of my hair. When I spun around, the weighted plaits swung around me in a wide circle. No one dared come close to me, for fear of being hit in the face with them. A grand weapon!

My mother came outside and saw me, and shouted, 'You could hurt someone, Aoife!'

'I'm not trying to hurt anyone, we're just having fun.'

Mother put her hands on her hips and scowled. 'Really, Aoife, I don't know what will become of you. Sometimes you're like a wild creature.'

But when she told Father the story, he laughed.

Chapter 2
RICHARD

Preparing for a Hard Life

I was christened Richard FitzGilbert de Clare, and my father had every reason to expect I would one day hold his title as Earl of Pembroke. But I was born into a hard time.

My earliest memories are of battle tales. Every detail of war was discussed in my father's hall until the firelight seemed to reflect blood-red on the walls. I had bad dreams at night, and thought the world was filled with death and killing. I never felt safe.

'You still don't look much like a warrior,' my father said after my legs lengthened and I became tall. 'You have a womanish face. And all those freckles. Your skin should be hard and brown from being out in all weathers, not dappled like an egg. Like a child's. And your voice! Why hasn't your voice changed? Why am I cursed with a son who has a high voice?'

'I can't make my voice change,' I told him. 'I would if I could, but I can't.'

'You do it to annoy me,' he said coldly.

It was important to my father that I be a warrior like himself. 'Our family won their lands fighting against the savage Welsh,' he often reminded me. 'We proved to be better warriors, we Normans. Your ancestors came to England with William the Conqueror, remember that, Richard. You bear a proud name. Your great-grandfather fought with William against the Saxons, and won. Now we fight in the king's name against the Welsh, and we win. We always win. Remember that, Richard. We are Normans, we always win.' His voice was as hard as flint. He believed what he was telling me.

'How can anyone win all the time?' I wondered.

But he didn't answer my question.

For a while, we did win against the Welsh. Fighting them was my father's whole life. My mother explained it to me. 'The King of England, King Stephen, has made your father Earl of Pembroke as a reward for his services in holding this land against the Welsh,' she told me. 'With the title, your father has been given a large grant of land, making us very wealthy.'

'But didn't that land belong to the Welsh before?' I wanted to know.

'It did, and they still want it back. The Welsh are strange people, Richard. They are Celts, and like the Irish Celts, they love the land for its own sake. To us it is property. To them it is something more than that.'

As Earl of Pembroke, my father was one of the Marcher lords, sworn to defend the western borders in the king's name. The western borderland was called the Welsh Marches.

'The name even sounds like soldiers and battle,' I said once to my father.

'Don't be fanciful,' he snapped.

I never said anything like that to him again.

My father had to fight more than the wild Welsh. The nobles of England were always fighting among themselves, too. Everyone wanted more power. It wasn't easy, choosing sides. If you chose the wrong side you could lose everything.

When I was only ten years old my father began saying to me, 'If I am ever killed in battle, Richard, it will be up to you to defend our property and our name. Remember that!'

Long before I was fifteen, which was the usual age for a boy to take up arms, he said to me, 'I made my name with the Welsh longbow. It's time you learned to use the same weapon. I am called Strongbow and you must be Strongbow after me, Richard.'

He didn't ask me if I wanted to be Strongbow. He was, so I must be.

'Can't I have a nickname of my own?' I asked my mother. It was easier to ask my mother things than to talk to my father. She listened to me.

'You must be proud to bear his name,' she told me. 'His family belongs to him, you know. I do, you do, we all do. Like his lands,' she added. 'That is the law.'

For the first time, I heard a sadness in my mother's voice. I wondered if she liked belonging to my father, like his lands and his horse. She was so gentle. Was it hard for her, being a warrior's wife?

But I couldn't ask her that.

Learning to use the longbow was very hard. I was too young, and didn't have enough strength. I did my best, but it wasn't good enough.

'You aren't trying, Richard!' my father yelled at me. 'You disgrace me!'

'I am trying,' I insisted. 'I'm doing my best.'

'Then your best isn't good enough,' he said coldly. He turned his back and walked away. That hurt worse than his yelling at me.

I tried harder.

Sometimes the bowstring tore the skin from my fingers. It felt as if I had put my hand into fire. I sucked my fingers to draw out the pain, and ran to my mother. 'Poor little lad,' she always said. If my father wasn't around, she would take me into her arms and comfort me.

'I'll sing you a song about Normandy,' she said. 'A song about warm summers and blue skies, the way Normandy was in my girlhood. Would you like that, my little lad?' She kissed my hurt fingers and stroked my hair and sang, and the pain eased.

Our castle was cold and dark, with thick stone walls and narrow slits for shooting arrows out at the enemy. The castle wasn't supposed to be comfortable. It was built to defend us, to defend England from the wild Welsh. It was one of the Marcher castles that were set all along the border with Wales. My mother hated it.

'There are no flowers here,' she'd say.

But Father wouldn't let her have gardens. 'To tend gardens you would have to be in the open,' he said, 'and it isn't safe to be in the open. A spear could come over even the highest wall.'

Our castle had a keep, a safe place, in its centre, with a hall and chambers where we slept. It had high walls and towers where soldiers took turns day and night, watching for the enemy. We all learned to think about the enemy more than we thought about each other. Every day I imagined the eyes of the wild Welsh, watching us from the mountains.

I was told terrible stories about them. 'The Celtic people are savages,' my father said many times. 'They should all be slain to make the land safe for civilised people.'

But my mother told me, 'The Welsh are not monsters, Richard. The maidservant who takes care of my clothing is half Welsh, and you couldn't find a sweeter girl.'

She summoned the maidservant. 'Sing for Richard,' she said.

The girl blushed and stared at her feet. 'I can only sing a little, but I can say poetry.'

'Say it then,' my mother ordered.

And so I heard for the first time the language of the wild Welsh, and it was sweet and beautiful, like water running over stones.

My mother was proud of her servant. 'She can read and write,' she told me.

'Read? And write?' I was astonished. I didn't know anyone who could read and write, except the priests. It seemed a magical thing to me, a gift from God. My mother thought so too. 'I wish I could read a little, so I could read my prayer book,' she confided in me.

'Would Father let you learn?'

She was shocked. 'Your father cannot read. He would certainly not want me to. That's not a woman's place.'

Yet a Welsh servant could do it. I puzzled over this. Perhaps, I thought in my bed at night, God was on the side of the Welsh. Perhaps that was why they were beginning to win against the Marcher lords from time to time.

When they had some small victory my father despised them more than ever.

Not all of the Normans hated the Welsh as much as my father did. Some Normans even married Welsh women. But when Father saw me talking to mother's maidservant he took me out into the courtyard and beat me.

'Don't ever do that again!' he shouted at me. 'They're savages. You're better than they are.'

Then he got rid of the woman. I never knew how. He owned her, he could do anything he liked with her.

Afterwards, my mother began to fade away. Her face got very thin and there were dark rings under her eyes. Then they kept her shut up in her chamber and I wasn't allowed to see her, though I waited outside all day in the cold passageway.

At last someone came out and told me I had a baby sister.

Then Father came, looking like a thundercloud. 'A miserable girl,' was all he could say. He stalked past me without even looking at me.

Once he was gone, the servants let me go in and see my mother.

She was so pale she frightened me. 'You will have to love your little sister enough to make up to her for not having a father's love, Richard,' she told me. Her voice was no more than a whisper.

I grabbed her hand and held it tight. It was very cold. 'How can I do that, Mother?'

'With all your heart, Richard. With all your heart.'

Shortly after my baby sister was christened Basilia, my mother died. I don't know what killed her.

Perhaps it was just a lack of flowers.

Life was harder for me after that. I had to practise fighting all the time. Father assigned me a training master who taught me to use the sword and ride a horse. At first I didn't like horses. I was put onto a giant black animal with huge legs, and the ground was so far away my mouth went dry. When the horse started to move I couldn't make it stop and I cried out.

The training master took me off the horse and beat me with a strap. Then he put me back in the saddle. I didn't cry out again.

In time, I learned to ride. I think the horse felt sorry for me. But as soon as we became friends, it was taken away and I was given another one, bigger, harder to ride, and the training went on.

At night I crept into bed, aching all over.

Sometimes I went first to the nursery where my baby sister lived. It helped to visit her before I went to sleep. It helped to hold her in my arms – while her nurse watched and frowned, afraid I'd drop her.

'Basilia,' I whispered, 'I'm sore and tired and afraid. But I can't tell anybody. Except you.'

She smelled sweet, the way babies do, and she always smiled at me and waved her little hands. She was as gentle as our mother had been. She might not understand my words, but she knew I loved her.

I loved her with all my heart. Basilia was my friend, my safe place.

By the time I was fourteen I had hands as hard as cured leather. I was nothing but muscle and bone, and the muscles were hard, too. I went to bed afraid and woke up afraid. At night I was afraid the Welsh would attack us while we slept, and in the morning I was afraid of the training master.

When I was fifteen, my father took me to my first battle.

We were trying to sneak up on a company of Welshmen in a deep, narrow valley near the border. Great dark pine trees marched like soldiers up the slopes on either side. In my memory I can still smell them. Their smell was sweet, like the smoke coming from the enemy's cooking fire.

They didn't know we were closing in on them. My father was in the lead, on his horse, with the rest of us on foot following him. When his scouts told him the Welsh were half a mile away, he dismounted and walked with us.

'Will there be a big battle?' I asked him. My heart was beating very fast.

'I hope so.' His voice was cold and grim. 'It's time you learned about battle.'

There were two score of us, I think – forty men or so. But suddenly I felt alone. I tried to move closer to my father. He shrugged his shoulder as if he wanted to shake me off. 'Don't crowd me,' he said. 'I need space around me to use my weapons.'

I dropped back a step, but he turned around and I could feel him glaring at me, even if I couldn't see his face. I couldn't see anyone's face. We all wore heavy iron helmets that covered our noses and cheekbones and had slits like arrowslits for our eyes.

'Stay in the front line!' my father barked at me. His voice echoed inside his helmet. 'Don't fall back like a coward! And whatever happens, Richard, follow my banner!'

We began making our way among the trees. Sometimes I couldn't see the banner, or the man who was carrying it for Father. I was afraid

Father would yell at me for losing sight of it.

It was hot inside the helmet, though the day was cold. Sweat ran down my forehead and into my eyes, making them sting. But I couldn't take off the helmet to wipe it away.

Then, through the slits, I had my first sight of the enemy. The wild Welsh. They were sitting around a campfire, and a deer was roasting on the spit. My mouth watered. We hadn't yet eaten our daily meal, and I was always hungry.

The Welsh looked up and saw us. They jumped to their feet and ran for their weapons, which were piled near the fire.

Our men ran forward, yelling. I had a sword in my hand and I yelled too, but my feet didn't want to run forward. More than anything else, I wanted to turn around and run back into the shadowy safety of the trees. But I was afraid to run away because Father would do something terrible to me.

My heart was pounding so hard I thought it would burst out of my body. I was hot and cold at the same time, and my skin prickled all over. I knew I would be scared. I didn't know I would be this scared. It felt like the hair was standing up on my head, inside my helmet. My stomach heaved.

Our men were making so much noise I couldn't think. My feet acted on their own. They started to run forward with the other men. I couldn't help myself. I was caught up in it, doing what everyone else was doing. My running feet carried me, terrified, straight towards the enemy. Men on either side of me were shoving and screaming and I screamed too. I don't know what I said, I just screamed.

We burst out of the trees and a Welsh warrior stepped right in front of me.

At first his face was only a pale blur. Then I saw he was a boy not much older than myself. He didn't even have a beard yet, though the Welsh wear beards because they're savages.

He looked as frightened as I was. His eyes were huge and round and very dark blue. I remember those eyes still. I'll never forget them.

He had a spear in his hand, and I had a sword. We stood facing each other while the men fought around us. I wonder if he wanted to run off into the trees, the way I did.

Then I heard my father scream my name. 'Richard!' he cried. 'Kill him!'

I didn't dare think any more. I held tight to the hilt of my sword and ran it through the Welsh boy.

He didn't try to spear me. He didn't do anything but look at me with those great blue eyes. And then he fell.

He was just a lad like me.

My mouth tasted sour. I wanted to be sick. I ran away into the trees then, and no one tried to stop me.

My father found me later. 'Today you're a man,' he said.

Chapter 3
AOIFE

An Insult to the King of Brefni

My sister Urla liked to pretend she knew more than anybody else. She was older than me, and she spied on people and told tales. I didn't always believe the stories Urla told. I thought she made some of them up to make herself seem important.

One day she came to me with a gleam in her eyes like a stoat stealing eggs. She was still angry about the pony, I think. 'I know something you don't know,' she chanted.

I tossed my head. 'Why should I care?' I turned my back on her.

'Because it's about Father!' Urla hissed.

I paused. 'What about Father?'

'He did something very wicked once.'

'You're lying. I'll tell my mother.'

'I swear on the Holy Family that it's the truth.' Urla said solemnly. I had to listen, then. She would never have sworn such an oath for a lie.

'It began a long time ago,' she went on. 'A very long time ago …'

'Tell it!' I said. I was losing patience with Urla. She liked to drag out a story too much and I was always in a hurry.

Urla sat down on a bench and folded her hands. I sat beside her. 'When Father was sixteen years old,' she said. 'Turlough O'Connor was King of Connacht – and also claimed the high kingship of Ireland.

21

'Father's father was King of Leinster, but he died. His enemies killed him and buried a dog in his grave with him, as an insult. Then Father was supposed to become King of Leinster, but Turlough O'Connor wanted one of his own sons to rule Leinster instead. There was a war about it.'

'I should think so! And Father won. He's King of Leinster now and has been for a long time.'

'He is,' Urla agreed, 'but it took many years and many battles. One of the men who fought on the side of O'Connor, against Father, was Tiernan O'Rourke, the King of Brefni. O'Rourke killed most of the cattle in Leinster and burned the houses. He even burned Father's home here at Ferns. O'Connor and O'Rourke wanted to make Father feel so small and helpless that he'd never even try to be king.'

No wonder Father looked so sad sometimes, and sat staring into space with his chin on his fist. 'How did he ever win over them?' I wanted to know.

Urla's eyes danced. I never knew anyone who enjoyed telling awful things as much as Urla did. 'About three years later, when O'Connor and O'Rourke were fighting in some other part of Ireland, Father took revenge.

'Father's aunt had been Abbess of Kildare, but O'Connor had made one of his own kinswomen abbess instead. So when his enemies were busy elsewhere, Father raised an army and broke into the abbey. He looted it, and he hurt the abbess very badly. That was his wicked deed.'

'He'd never!' I cried.

'Ah but he did. I swear it. Then he made a woman of his own clan abbess. People were afraid of him after that. O'Connor and O'Rourke left him alone to be King of Leinster. But they never stopped trying to make trouble for him. Particularly O'Rourke, who hated him.

'Then Father struck a terrible blow against O'Rourke. A few years before you were born, Aoife, Father stole O'Rourke's wife.'

Now I was sure she was lying. 'How could you say such things about Father?' I shouted at Urla. 'You're an awful person and I'm glad Father gave me the pony instead of you, because I know he can't love you at all!' I whirled away from her and ran before she could hit me.

I ran straight into the arms of my half-brother, Donal Mac Murrough Kavanaugh. 'Here, what's this about?' he wanted to know.

Sobbing with anger, I told him. He listened to me with a grave expression on his face. 'Urla told you the truth,' he said at last. 'Father did indeed steal O'Rourke's wife. At least, he took her away from Brefni. I was here when he brought her to Ferns.'

'You were?'

'I was indeed. He rode through the gates with her slung across his horse, and his men-at-arms following them, laughing and winking at one another. As she came into the courtyard the woman pretended to scream, so people would believe she had been taken against her will. But she didn't scream very loudly and no one believed her. She and Father were too friendly. He gave her one of the best chambers and kept her here for a year or two, in great comfort.'

'What did his wives say about it?' I wanted to know.

'They didn't like it very much, nor did they like the woman, who was called Dervorgilla. But Father never offered to marry her, so they put up with her. Most of the Leinster folk approved of what Father had done. O'Rourke had insulted him, so he had returned the insult in full measure. And he never even paid O'Rourke an honour price for his stolen wife, which Father should have done under the law. It was a mighty insult to the King of Brefni and we thought he deserved it.

'Of course, it made O'Rourke hate Father more than ever. But Father was never afraid of him. When Turlough O'Connor died, an Ulster king called Mac Loughlin won the high kingship and Father made friends with him. So now he has as an ally the most powerful king in Ireland, and he's safe from O'Rourke.'

'What happened to Dervorgilla?' I wanted to know, relieved to hear that Father was safe.

Donal laughed. 'Oh, after a time she and Father fell out and she went away. I think she went into a convent somewhere.'

Poor Dervorgilla, I thought. And then I forgot about her, which was a mistake.

Because Dervorgilla was not forgotten in Ireland.

By stealing her, Father had made O'Rourke hate him more than ever. Hate him enough to destroy him utterly, to become a deadly foe who would never rest until he saw my father in his grave. O'Rourke had become a man who would stop at nothing to hurt my father. And his family.

I did not know, then, that we were all living under the shadow of Dervorgilla.

That night in the hall I studied my father's face closely. He had made people fear him by acting brutally. That was not the man I knew. When he pretended to be a bear and growl at me, that was only play. Could there be a real bear hidden in my father somewhere? I wondered.

I stood in the shadows beyond the central hearth and watched his face in the leaping firelight. He was a very large man, I realised, and very strong. His cheekbones were like boulders, his nose was hooked and his jaw was heavy. How strange it was to know that other people were afraid of him! And yet, watching him, I could imagine that he might frighten people who didn't know him.

Then he saw me watching him, and winked at me.

After that, whenever Father rode away I knew he was going to do brave deeds and wonderful things in defense of Leinster. He had won the kingship against strong enemies, and was willing to fight anyone to keep it. He had even rebuilt Ferns after the wicked Tiernan O'Rourke destroyed it, and now our home was fine and grand, surely better than it had been before.

He could do anything, my father.

How I envied Donal Mac Murrough Kavanaugh, who was old enough to fight at his side!

It didn't seem too fair to me that girls weren't allowed to do all the things boys could do.

'Why aren't girls allowed to go to war?' I asked my mother.

She threw up her hands. 'Who on earth puts such ideas into your head, Aoife?'

'No one does. I just want to know why I can't be a warrior like Father or Donal.'

My mother sighed. 'Because women don't fight.'

This was not exactly true. 'But you fight with Urla's mother,' I reminded her.

She sighed again. 'That's different. We merely argue. I'm Dermot's second wife and it would be wrong of me to fight with his senior wife. Especially since the senior wife has to give permission for a second wife to marry her husband. Mor gave that permission, so I try hard to be friends with her.'

'I try to be friends with Urla,' I said, 'but sometimes we fight. So why can't women fight in real battles?'

'You don't know what you're talking about, Aoife. War is dreadful, it's not a game played by children in a courtyard. Men suffer and die for nothing, because almost as soon as one battle is over another begins.

'Only during the reign of Brian Boru as High King was there a time of peace in Ireland, but that ended with his death. Now the battles go on as before.'

'If Father were High Hing, he would make people keep the peace,' I said. 'I know he would.'

Mother stared at me. 'Your father? Bring peace? That's your oddest idea yet.'

'Why? Isn't he a good king?'

'Dermot is a good king – for Leinster,' Mother had to agree. 'Since he began his reign there have been rich harvests every season, and the cattle are fat in the fields. If anyone tries to take what belongs to us your father drives them away. His strong sword arm, and his reputation, keep us safe here. Scholars even come long distances to study in the great library he built here in Ferns, and he endowed a new monastery here for the Augustinians.

'Indeed, your father is a good king for Leinster. But for many reasons, Aoife, I can't imagine him being High King of Ireland. He has too many enemies.

'If anything ever happens to your father's friend Mac Loughlin the High King, Dermot's enemies will come down on him again like wolves onto a lamb.'

'He can fight them off,' I said confidently. 'I know he can.'

'I hope you're right,' said my mother. 'But someday he must surely grow tired. His entire life has been a battle, and no man can go on forever.'

My father could, I thought.

I continued to play at war in the courtyard with the boys. I continued to push stones into the plaits of my hair and swing my head to keep my enemies at bay.

I was Dermot Mac Murrough's daughter. Aoife Rua, they called me. Red Eva.

Chapter 4
RICHARD

Kings Have Ways of Getting Even

Because I'd killed a man in battle, my father saw me differently.

'Your childhood is over,' he told me. 'You're still thin and gawky, but from now on you'll live a man's life. You'll be given better weapons, and armour for a grown man, and I expect you to do honour to both.'

'Will the armour fit me?' I wondered, looking at my bony body.

'Not at first. You'll grow into it.'

He didn't care if the armour rubbed and chafed, and I knew it would do no good to complain. I would just have to grow.

Getting used to wearing armour took a long time. It was terribly heavy, and stiff. You had to learn a whole new way of moving. Each morning when I dressed, with the help of a squire, I put on a woollen tunic padded with old rags. Over this I wore a shirt of chain mail, tiny links of iron joined together. It looked like knitted fabric from a distance, but it wasn't. It rubbed my skin even through the padded tunic. A coif, or hood, of chain mail went over my head to protect my ears and the back of my neck. When the sun shone on this coif the metal grew hot and blistered my cheeks.

The coat of mail reached almost to my knees, with an opening at the front and another at the back so I could mount a horse. Armour made me so heavy my squire had to push me up into the saddle, and the horse laid his ears back at the noise the metal made. As I had killed a man I was given a new helmet as a reward, one fitted with a face guard. This was even hotter than the helmet I had before. It didn't make me feel more safe, only less comfortable.

Some Norman knights had solid plates of armour strapped to their chests and backs to protect them, but my father didn't approve of this fashion.

'It makes a man as helpless as a shell makes a turtle,' he said. He thought the ability to move was more important than being shielded from blows.

My squire, a youth called Roland, admired my armour. But he didn't have to wear it, he only had to keep it oiled and ready for me. Sometimes I saw him looking at me as if he thought he could do better justice to armour than I could.

I didn't trust him. I didn't trust anyone, as my father had taught me.

'Always guard your back,' Father said. 'Everyone is after you. No man is safe. Be watchful.'

He wasn't watchful enough, however.

I was at the castle when a messenger on a sweating horse galloped into the courtyard. The man's eyes were wild. 'Gilbert de Clare is dead!' he cried as if he couldn't believe it. 'Strongbow is dead!'

One of the servants dropped a bucketful of water. I heard it clattering on the cobblestones. I felt as if the cold water had been thrown on me.

We learned in bits and pieces of how he died, as his men came straggling back to the castle. He had been in a skirmish, a small battle on the border, and some whispered he had been killed by one of his own men.

'He was hated,' I was told by Father's own squire. 'The great lords are often hated by their people. You'll learn that for yourself.'

'I will?'

'You're the lord here now. It will be up to you to hold the de Clare castle and defend your share of the Welsh Marches.'

No sooner had he said this than people started bowing to me, knuckling their forelocks as I passed by. At first it made me want to laugh. I felt like I was pretending to be someone I was not. But I couldn't laugh. I was supposed to be mourning my father.

Did I mourn him? I don't remember. I must have done. I should have done. He was my father, the great de Clare.

But all too soon I learned just what sort of man he had been. I was shocked to discover that he died owing a great amount of money to a great number of people. Men seemed to come from the farthest corners of the kingdom with their hands out. 'De Clare promised me this,' they'd say. 'De Clare owed me that. You must pay.'

I couldn't even ride out with a falcon on my wrist to go hunting without having a creditor approach me. They had no shame, they were not noble. They ran after me, yelling. They threw themselves in front of my horse.

Father would have trampled such men beneath the hooves of his horse, but I couldn't. I stopped and talked to them. I made promises I didn't know how to keep, but I was always courteous.

They thought, because I had fine features like a woman's, that I was soft. I wasn't soft. I was simply my mother's son, and she had taught me good manners before she died.

That's all I have left of her now. That, and my sister, Basilia.

With my parents dead, I became the guardian of my infant sister. I wanted to give her a good life. She would be a Norman noblewoman, she should have fine gowns to wear and jewels, and there should be lute-players in her chamber, making music for her all the day.

I longed for music, myself. For the life of the wealthy. For a garden with flowers. But all that took money. Property. Power.

The struggle for power was growing in England, between old King Stephen and young Henry Plantagenet. Because Stephen had been my father's friend, I took his side.

I sold my sword in Stephen's service and helped to fight his battles wherever I was needed. Thus I took up the career which had been my father's, the only career possible for a Norman knight. I became a professional warrior.

It was a hard life. Battle after battle, and long treks in the saddle. It made me a hard man. There was little time in my life then for music and flowers.

Whenever I could, I returned to my castle to see Basilia. I needed to know that she was safe and happy. As soon as I got home I'd rush up to the small high room at the top of the tower, the safest room in the castle. It was my sister's nursery. Her nurse would tiptoe out and leave us together.

Even when she was a baby, Basilia always had a smile for me. She wrapped her tiny fingers around one of my big ones the way she wrapped herself around my heart. No matter how bad my day had been, when I saw Basilia I felt better. All the hardness inside me melted away.

I took her in my arms and pressed my cheek against her silky hair. 'My sister,' I whispered to her. The pale strands of her hair felt like silk threads to my rough hands. 'My sister. Blood of my blood. We have other kinfolk, Basilia, but they live elsewhere and I rarely see them. Only you and I are our mother's children. You would have loved her. You are so much like her.'

It was true. Basilia was small and frail and gentle like our mother. When I was with her, I could be gentle too. 'I don't have to pretend to be fierce and warlike when I'm with you,' I told her. 'That would frighten you. But I have to be very different outside this chamber. I must defend our name and property, so the world has to believe I'm a hard man like my father.'

Once, and only once, I made the mistake of forgetting to take off my armour before I went to see Basilia. She shrieked aloud at the sight of me in my helmet. After that I was always very careful to remove my battle gear first, so I could go to her with my face washed and no blood on my hands.

As time passed, there was often blood on my hands. Beyond Basilia's chamber the world was full of war.

People began calling me by my father's nickname: Strongbow.

Basilia was learning to talk. She called me 'Wichad'.

'I have another name now,' I told her. 'I am Father's heir, Earl of Pembroke and also Earl of Strigul. I have power and position, Basilia. I'm somebody important, can you imagine? Men follow my banner now, and I have a reputation as a warrior. I don't enjoy fighting very much, but no one knows that. Except you. They call me Strongbow now,' I told her. 'That's my name now.'

Basilia laughed and clapped her little hands.

'Stwongbow!' she said.

It sounded better when she said it. I found I liked the name. I was proud to be Basilia's 'Stwongbow'.

As my sister was growing up, Stephen, King of England, was growing old and weak. He wanted his son Eustace to be king after him. I supported Eustace because I didn't want Henry Plantagenet, who was usually away in France, to rule England. But then Eustace died. His death broke his father's heart. Within a year King Stephen was dead, and Henry Plantagenet returned in triumph to become King Henry II of England.

Henry didn't forget the names of those who had not wanted him to be king. The name of the Earl of Pembroke was on that list. My name.

Kings have ways of getting even.

I was a nobleman with titles and land and a castle, but in truth I was very poor. My father's debts took years to pay off. Even when that was done, I could not seem to make money. The land should have supported us well, I had tenants who were good farmers.

But as I told Basilia, 'When I demand that my tenants pay me my share of their crops, they say they can't. They tell me they have sick wives or sick children or their crop failed.'

'Is it true?' Basilia asked.

'I don't know,' I said miserably. 'I can't make myself call a man a liar to his face. And I can't throw him off the land if his family is sick. Father would have, but I can't. So there's no money for new clothes for you this year, little sister.'

'I don't mind,' Basilia said loyally.

But I knew she did. Girls like pretty things. And I needed things myself, fresh horses, new armour, food and pay for the men who followed my banner.

'Basilia,' I said to my sister one day, 'I've made up my mind. I'm going to have to marry a woman whose family will give her a good dowry. With dowry money I can pay my bills.'

'Who will you marry?'

'I've heard of a woman called Isabella who belongs to a family that is always eager to add more noble titles to its line. I think her father would be pleased to wed her to the Earl of Pembroke. I'll ask him for her.'

I never doubted I would get her. Men married off their daughters for many reasons, and the daughters could not object. Women belonged to their men. That was our law.

Basilia belonged to me. Someday, when she was older, I could marry her to a wealthy man and improve my lot that way.

Isabella's father agreed to the marriage and gave her a large dowry, which made things easier for me, for a while.

Isabella was not pretty, nor was she sweet. She was only rich.

'I'm afraid I don't like your wife very much,' Basilia once

admitted to me. 'She doesn't like me.'

'Nonsense. Everyone likes a pretty little girl.'

'Not Isabella. She thinks you spend too much time with me,' my sister said. She was very wise for her years.

So I tried to spend more time with my wife, but in truth, I had very little time to spare. I was involved in various struggles, some against the wild Welsh and some against my own countrymen, just as my father had been.

And I was on the wrong side.

I shall never forget the look in my wife's eyes on the day the messenger came to us from King Henry's court, to tell me I was no longer Earl of Pembroke. That title, and the lands that went with it, had been stripped from me by the king.

Isabella looked at me as if I was something scraped off her shoe.

'But I still have a title,' I tried to assure her. 'I am also Earl of Strigul. Henry hasn't taken that from me.'

'A minor title with very little land,' my wife said with a sniff. 'You've been a fool, Richard. Why didn't you support Henry? Look at Robert FitzHarding. He shouted his loyalty to Henry from the treetops, and now he's being showered with gifts and lands. You're reduced to nothing.'

'I'm not reduced to nothing,' I argued.

But she was so angry she wouldn't talk to me.

Keeping my face set so no one would know my true feelings, I went to Basilia's chamber. My sister was eight or nine years old at the time, old enough to know something was wrong. She put her hand in mine. 'What is it?' she asked gently.

To my horror, I felt tears in my eyes.

Basilia sat beside me on the window seat and held my hand. I could think of nothing to say. I didn't try to explain politics to her. I wanted to shield my sister from what went on beyond the castle walls.

But she would not be put off. 'Please tell me what's wrong,' she pleaded.

'I've lost the title,' I said at last.

She stared at me. 'You're not Strongbow any more?'

She wasn't thinking of the earldom. That meant nothing to her. She was thinking of the title I had worked so hard to earn for myself.

Instead of crying, I found myself laughing. How good it felt! I hardly ever laughed in those days. I put my arms around Basilia and hugged her tightly. 'It's all right,' I said. 'Don't worry. The title I lost is just one that kings can give.

'But I shall always be Strongbow.'

Chapter 5
AOIFE

Urla's Wedding

Our father didn't give his children out to fosterage. He could have done so, most Irish kings did. Having their children raised in other powerful families was supposed to form bonds of friendship. Father himself had been fostered by an O'Kelly chieftain in Ossory and he remained close to his foster parents all his life. But he didn't do the same with his own children. I think he loved us too much to be parted from us, even if it was the custom. The sons and daughters of his wives all grew up at Ferns, and so we saw everything that happened.

Father made sure that each of us was fitted for the life to come. Urla, as the oldest daughter, would be married first, and so she had the finest wardrobe. I would be married too, one day. Donal was trained to be a fine warrior, like Father. Enna, because he was sickly, didn't have to learn to fight, but was encouraged to be a great scholar. The youngest son, Conor, was given his own herd of cattle so he would have a fine rank as cattle-lord.

I remember Urla's wedding day. How she fussed and preened! She was like a chicken who has got its feathers wet and must put every one into order again.

'Everything has to be perfect,' she kept saying. 'I am, after all, marrying Donal O'Brien, son of Turlough, King of Thomond, whose grandfather's grandfather was Brian Boru!'

Brian Boru, greatest High King of Ireland. We had all heard the name, and the tales told of the man. For once I was almost jealous of Urla, marrying into such a family.

Then I thought of Father, who would make just as good a High King if he had the chance.

Perhaps he will now, I said to myself. Now that we have a link with the powerful O'Briens, the rulers of Munster, Father is stronger than ever. Maybe that's why he makes so many trips to Munster, to Thomond.

Laurence O'Toole himself married Urlacam and Donal. The great hall at Ferns blazed with hundreds of beeswax candles. Nobles came from everywhere to attend the wedding. The feasting and music would go on for days, and our servants were kept busy preparing all sorts of wonderful food.

I stood outside the kitchens and sniffed the air. Roast boar, roast venison, crisp brown fat ducks … I wondered when we children would be fed. Surely the noble guests would eat first, and get all the best parts. My stomach growled in protest.

Then my brother Conor tugged at my arm. Turning around, I saw he was holding a bulging sack. 'What's that, Conor?'

He grinned. 'A little something for us. I took it when no one was looking.'

He opened the neck of the sack and I peered inside. It was crammed full of meat and cheese and dark brown bread, and fruits like jewels, and even a pot of honey-custard made with cream and eggs.

I clapped my hands over my mouth to keep from shrieking with delight.

The two of us slipped off into the woods to enjoy our private feast. I knew of an old oak tree with a hollow at the base, where we could hide what we weren't able to eat. We sat crosslegged on the ground beneath the oak and stuffed ourselves until the grease ran down our chins.

'We must save something for Enna,' I reminded Conor. Poor Enna was sick again, lying in his chamber away from all the celebrations. After a little discussion we decided to save him half a roast duck, some of the fruit, and part of the pot of custard.

While we were gobbling our food we heard voices calling us. 'Conor? Aoife! Where are you?'

We didn't answer. We just ate faster, in case they were looking for us to punish us and take the food back.

But no one came to find us. We stayed in our hiding place until we couldn't swallow another bite. Then, slowly, we got up and made our way back toward Father's palace.

On the way, Conor groaned and put a hand to his belly. 'I don't feel very well,' he said.

I knew what he meant. I didn't feel very well, either.

Donal Mac Murrough Kavanaugh saw us coming and ran forward to meet us. 'Where have you been? Father wanted you. He had all of his children except you two sitting at the wedding table with Urla and her new husband!'

Conor and I looked at one another. We could have been sitting with the bride and groom, sharing all the choicest foods!

Our mother came up behind Donal and took one look at us. Our faces, and the stains on our clothes, told the story.

'You greedy children, you should be punished,' she said.

But just then Conor bent over and was sick. Very sick. A moment later, the same thing happened to me.

Donal laughed. He had a laugh very like Father's. 'Oh, I don't think you need to punish them, Sive,' he said. 'They'll suffer enough. They've done it to themselves.'

And so we had. We didn't get to any part of the wedding celebration, because we spent the next two days lying on our beds, sicker than Enna. We could hear music playing and people laughing and talking, but we didn't feel like joining them. And for several days, neither of us could stand the smell of roast meat.

Urla and her new husband left for Thomond, the most powerful kingdom in Munster. They wouldn't live in Brian Boru's great palace of Kincora, because that had been destroyed by Turlough O'Connor when he was High King. The O'Connors and the O'Briens continued to war on one another. But Urla would live in a fine new O'Brien stronghold and add children to the O'Brien clan, and Father was very pleased.

'It's a strong new link for us,' he told me, smiling.

Two other important events took place soon after. Donal Mac Murrough Kavanaugh married also, and Laurence O'Toole, Mor's brother, became Archbishop of Dublin.

Father celebrated by founding the monastery of All Hallows on land of his at Baldoyle, and giving other lands for the monastery of St Benedict.

Surely, I thought to myself, he has now made up for whatever sin he committed at Kildare? Now God must forgive him.

But I was wrong. Our days of peace and celebrating were almost over.

In Thomond, Murtough O'Brien, Urla's new brother-in-law, revolted against his own father and seized the kingship. The deposed king sought shelter in Leinster, the homeland of his son Donal's new wife. So it was that old Turlough O'Brien came to Ferns. Father took him in and treated him as an honoured guest.

He even gave O'Brien the chamber that once, according to rumour, had belonged to Dervorgilla.

Chapter 6
RICHARD

Death of a Wife

My wife gave me a son, whom I named Gilbert, for my father. Then we had a daughter called Isabella, for her mother. Children should have brought light and happiness to my castle. But they didn't.

'What good is having sons who won't inherit great titles?' my wife complained when Gilbert was born. After Isabella came, she moaned, 'We'll never be able to give her a good dowry, you're so poor. We'll be disgraced.'

From the day I ceased to be Earl of Pembroke, my wife had been unhappy. Nothing pleased her. If it rained she wanted sunshine. If the sun shone she longed for rain. She did not teach my children to love me. 'Your father is a failure,' she told them. Often.

She had to be my wife, but I could not make her love me. Only Basilia loved me. If it hadn't been for my sister, I would never have gone home. I would have lived the life of a wandering knight, travelling with only his squire and his horse for company, fighting in the service of anyone who would pay him.

Basilia was the only person I could talk to. 'Mine is not a happy family,' I admitted to her. 'My castle is full of long faces.'

'If my face is long,' she replied, 'it's because I worry about you. You fight too much, you risk your life all the time.'

'Fighting is my life, Basilia. How else can I hope to restore the fortune of the de Clares?'

'Marry me to a wealthy husband,' my sister suggested. 'Then I'll ask him to give you money and help you get back in favour with the king.'

I had to smile. She was so innocent. 'Men marry to strengthen their position, Basilia. Marrying my sister would not strengthen any man's position. Besides, you're not old enough to marry.'

I couldn't bear to think of losing her. She was the only light in my life.

Sometimes, riding away from the castle, I would turn and look back. The walls were grey and grim, the battlements looked like dragons' teeth against the sky. Rooks wheeled in the air like birds of ill omen. Enemies were everywhere. Friends were thin on the ground.

A cold lump of loneliness and sadness lay in my belly. There must be something better than this somewhere, I thought to myself. Somewhere. There must be.

As Earl of Strigul I still had a few men-at-arms, and with this small force I hired myself out to whoever would pay me. I helped my neighbours fight back the Welsh. My armour grew more dented; my body was covered with scars. My hair turned grey. Lines cobwebbed my face. I could feel myself growing old, and I knew I had never been young.

A warrior's life is hard and contains no music, no flowers. But it was all I knew. I was a middle-aged man with no happiness to look forward to. Only endless battles. I'm sorry to say that in my sadness, I wasted what little money I made.

One dark autumn day I returned to my castle to find the servants very upset. 'Your lady wife is dying,' they told me.

I ran to her chamber. There she lay on the bed, her face very pale. I knelt beside her.

'I didn't know you were ill,' I told her, 'or I would have come home sooner.'

She looked at me with eyes that did not seem to see me. 'I didn't send word to you,' she said in a whisper, 'because what could you do?'

What could I do, indeed? I was a big, strong man, but I was useless as far as my wife was concerned.

I sat beside her bed with bowed head, and held her hand as she died. The cold lump in my belly grew heavier and heavier. Basilia was crying. My children were crying. But I must never cry. I was a knight, and a Norman. I must be strong and stern.

I left my wife's deathbed and went to stare out the narrow arrowslit at the tiny bit of land it revealed beyond the walls of the grey, grim castle.

Somewhere, there must be happy people, not like us, I thought.

With my wife dead, the care of my children fell upon my sister and the servants. I saw Basilia becoming thin and tired. It was wrong for her to devote her whole life to us. She was young, she should have a husband one day soon, and children of her own. But who would marry the sister of a knight who was out of favour with the king? I must find someone for her!

I had a scribe write a letter to Henry for me, pledging my loyalty to him and asking that he restore the earldom of Pembroke to me. He didn't answer.

The captain of my guard, a man called Raymond le Gros, saw Basilia in the courtyard one day and asked me about her. 'Has she a suitor? Has she a dowry? She's very pretty.'

Raymond was plump and strong, with curling hair and a big nose. A pleasant companion, a good leader of men, an outstanding fighter. But he had no title. I wanted a titled husband for my sister, a man who could protect her.

I didn't want to make Raymond angry, however, so I said, 'We can

41

discuss this later. Now is not a good time to be bargaining for Basilia. She's still a little too young.'

Raymond raised one eyebrow and his eyes went cold. Suddenly he did not look so pleasant. 'I see,' he said. 'You want someone better than me for her.'

'I didn't say that.'

'You thought it,' he replied. 'But I have prospects. I mean to make my fortune with my sword as other men do. I'll ask you for your sister again, you can count on it. I never let anything I want get away from me.'

His words sounded like a threat. I was not at all certain I liked the idea of marrying Basilia to Raymond. But what other prospects did she have?

It was just something more for me to worry about.

I approached King Henry's longtime friend, Robert FitzHarding, to ask him to speak to the king on my behalf. As one of the rewards for his loyalty, Henry had made FitzHarding the portreeve of the town of Bristol, which was a very important office. If anyone could persuade Henry to restore my title and estates to me, I thought FitzHarding was that man.

I told him my story as simply as I could. 'So you see I've lost everything,' I concluded, 'though I really had nothing against Henry Plantagenet. I was merely supporting the son of a friend of my father's. You have profited through your friendship with Henry. Surely I should not be punished for my own loyalties. Isn't loyalty to our friends a virtue?'

FitzHarding said nothing.

I grew desperate.

'Please,' I said. 'I have children. I must have something to leave them!'

The Portreeve of Bristol sat across the table from me, studying my face. I could tell that he was measuring me in his mind. Was I a man worthy of being restored to the king's favour? That was the question he was asking himself.

I met his eyes squarely, letting him see Strongbow, who was a strong man and respected warrior, a man worth befriending.

At last FitzHarding nodded, and favoured me with a smile like sunlight on snow. 'I'll do what I can for you. But tell me this. You're famed for your skill with bow and arrow, I believe?'

'I am,' I said proudly.

His eyebrows drew together. 'Are you aware that the Church banned the use of archery in wars against Christians thirty years ago?'

'We heard something to that effect, but no one paid much attention to it in the Welsh Marches. Or anywhere else, as far as I know. The bow is too good a weapon to set aside.'

FitzHarding's smile had vanished. 'King Henry's advisor, Thomas à Becket, has been made Archbishop of Canterbury and has spoken out strongly against ignoring canon law. You would be well advised to set aside your bow.'

To set aside my bow would mean to cease being Strongbow. How could I? Was that the price Henry would ask of me, in return for restoring me to his favour?

Sadly, I shook my head. 'I'm sorry,' I told FitzHarding, 'but I'm a warrior who was trained in a hard school, and one I can't forget. I cannot change.' Bowing my head to him in respect, and with regret, I rose and left the room.

'You're a man of integrity, at least,' I heard him say as I went out the door.

Had I made a mistake? I never knew when I was making mistakes, it was only afterwards that I would discover how wrong I had been. And I always seemed to be doing the wrong thing. Though he had been dead for years, I could still imagine my father's eyes on me, and feel his disappointment in me.

But he had been Strongbow. And so was I. I had that much at least, after all I had lost, and I would not give it up.

Chapter 7

AOIFE

Fire!

With Urla married and gone, and her father-in-law settled at Ferns under Dermot's protection, I thought life would go on much as before. I even began to dream of the day I would be getting married myself, for I was growing older and men's eyes were beginning to follow me.

'You're so tall, Aoife!' my little sister Dervla said admiringly. 'I wish I looked like you. I wish I had hair like yours, like a fire blazing.'

Aoife Rua. Red Aoife. I was tall, and good to look at, and I knew it. I would get a better husband than Urla had. I was looking forward to my future.

Then things started to go wrong. Terribly wrong.

First came the news that the High King, Mac Loughlin, was dead. Not only dead, but murdered by his enemies, who claimed he was not fit for the high kingship.

He was soon replaced by a prince of Connacht called Rory O'Connor – whose right-hand man was Tiernan O'Rourke!

I was in the great hall at Ferns the day the news came. When I heard the messenger's words, I felt a cold chill run across my shoulders as if a winter wind was blowing through an open doorway.

But it was summer.

Father listened to everything the messenger had to say, and asked a number of questions. Then he just sat on his high seat facing the doorway, with his chin on his fist. He stared into space and spoke to no one.

Everyone seemed afraid to approach him, but I went to him. 'What will happen now?' I asked him.

He turned his head very slowly until his eyes met mine. They were as dark as two cinders.

'It's in the hands of God,' he said.

His voice sounded hollow, as if he spoke from the bottom of a well.

'But God must love you,' I assured him. 'You've done so many good works. You founded monasteries, you took care of your people, and…'

Father raised his hand to stop my rushing words. 'No man can be certain of God's favour,' he said, 'who has done such things as I've done.'

It was the only time he ever spoke to me of the wicked deeds of his past.

The summer sun was very hot. The days grew steamy and hazy. A dull mist was caught in the tops of the grasses, and people yawned over their work. No one could recall such a hot summer in Leinster before.

My legs had grown so long that my feet dragged the ground when I sat on the golden Norse pony. So Father gave me a new horse, a shining bay with a white star on its forehead. I was riding my new horse through the woods north of Ferns one afternoon, trying to stay cool in the dappled shade, when a stray breeze brought me the smell of smoke.

I stopped my horse. I sniffed the air. Perhaps I was dreaming?

Then I smelled it again.

I turned my horse around and trotted back through the woods the way I had come. As I drew closer to Ferns I looked up and saw a black stain of smoke in the sky above the trees.

I kicked my horse in the ribs and raced for home.

When I burst out of the woods, I could see the flames.

A stray spark had lodged in the thatched roof of one of the many wattle-and-daub houses that crowded around the walls of our stronghold. Ferns was not only the seat of the King of Leinster, but a large village with a market square and many homes and workshops and storehouses. Except for our palace, the monastery and the church, all the buildings were of timber. The summer heat had made them very dry.

The fire raced through them, gobbling.

Everywhere I looked, thatch was ablaze. Sparks shot into the sky. A hot wind blew towards me, carrying them, and some touched my face like fingers of fire.

I galloped through the open gates of our stronghold and slid from my horse. People were running in every direction, trying to gather their families or drag their possessions from burning buildings or throw buckets of water, uselessly, on the fire.

The fire was too big and too angry. It only hissed at the touch of water, and grew stronger.

'Father!' I screamed. 'Father!'

I couldn't see him. I began running like the others, darting this way and that, sobbing with fear, calling his name. The fire roared as if it was alive. My insides cramped with terror.

'*Father*!'

Then I saw him coming towards me. His face was black with soot, his clothes were half burned off him. When he saw me, he ran forward and grabbed me in his arms.

'Thank God!' he cried. 'Now get out of here, Aoife. Run. Out the gates. Wait for me outside, and stay away from the fire, do you hear me?'

'But –'

For the only time in my life, my father hit me. He hit me on the side of the head with the flat of his hand, making my ears ring. 'Run!' he ordered.

I ran.

From a safe distance, I watched the people fight the fire. The battle was lost before it began. By the end of the day, Ferns had been destroyed a second time in Father's lifetime. Little was left but glowing coals and ashes, and the scorched stone walls of our palace and the monastery and church.

The people of Ferns had lost everything but their lives. By some miracle – perhaps because the fire took place in broad daylight – no one had been trapped and burned to death. But clothes and beds and tables were gone, and cattle and fowl had been roasted in their pens before anyone could get them out.

I shall never forget the way it smelled. The next morning I walked with Father through the ruins. He kept kicking bits of charred wood out of our way.

'We'll build again,' he said. 'Ferns will rise on these ruins, finer than before. You'll see, Aoife. You'll see.'

But his eyes were very sad. I wondered if he thought God was punishing him at last, for his wickedness.

Perhaps. But if that was so, there was much worse punishment yet to come.

Chapter 8
RICHARD

A Visitor from Ireland

I had made a friend of Robert FitzHarding, it seemed. Perhaps he felt sorry for me, an impoverished widower. From time to time he put a bit of business my way. He had me provide an armed guard for travelling merchants in the west, and helped me get a good price for horses and supplies for myself. I was grateful to him.

One day he sent a messenger to my castle, asking me to call upon him in Bristol. It sounded important. I hastily gathered a band of men-at-arms and had my squire polish my dented armour. Then we set out for the port city.

As we rode through its narrow streets towards the quays, I caught glimpses of a strange ship docked below. By the shape of it I knew it for a Norse longship, yet an Irish banner was flying from its masthead.

When I met Robert FitzHarding, he explained.

'The ship you saw belongs to the King of Leinster, in Ireland, who has just been here seeking my aid,' FitzHarding said.

'Why would an Irish king come to you? Is he in trouble?'

'Grave trouble. Dermot Mac Murrough has some powerful enemies, and they've done to him the worst thing anyone can do to a king.'

I was interested in hearing of any man who had worse trouble than I did. 'Tell me,' I said.

'Some years ago, Dermot stole the wife of another Irish king, a man called O'Rourke. There is a great hatred between Mac Murrough and O'Rourke, but for a time Mac Murrough was safe from O'Rourke because the High King of Ireland himself was a friend of Mac Murrough's. But then the old High King died and a new one took his place. He is Rory O'Connor of Connacht, and he's a great friend of O'Rourke's.

'O'Rourke applied to the new High King to punish Dermot Mac Murrough. Together they attacked the King of Leinster. He fought bravely against them, but his own people began to desert him. They said God was angry with him. At last he had only his own clansmen fighting on his side, and he was overcome by O'Connor and O'Rourke.'

'It's a bad thing to make an enemy of a king,' I said from my own experience.

FitzHarding nodded. 'The High King of Ireland stripped the kingship of the province of Leinster from Dermot Mac Murrough. He was left with his life, but little else.

'That's why he has come across the sea to England. He hopes to hire warriors here who will go to Ireland and fight for him, help him regain his kingship. Would you be interested, de Clare?'

I considered. Would I fight in Ireland, where I had never been, for a man I didn't know?

It couldn't be much worse than fighting the Welsh here. But I wasn't a young man any more, and I had responsibilities. My face must have told FitzHarding I was going to refuse.

FitzHarding held up his hand. 'Before you answer, let me tell you one thing more,' he said. 'Dermot Mac Murrough is about to leave Bristol and go in search of our king. He intends to ask Henry personally for an army.

'If King Henry gives the deposed King of Leinster such an army, would you be willing to be part of it?'

I had to stop and think. If our king decided to help this Dermot Mac Murrough, and I took part in that army, I would be doing Henry a service. I could get back in his good graces that way.

But I must be careful. I must know just which way the wind was blowing.

'Why should King Henry be willing to help Dermot Mac Murrough?' I wanted to know.

'Because when Mac Murrough still had power in Leinster, he once sent some Norse ships to attack the Welsh on their coast while Henry was fighting them from the front. It was the sort of favour one king may do another, and it has put our king in his debt.'

I understood about being in debt to someone. 'And what about you, Robert?' I asked my friend. 'Why do you want to help Dermot Mac Murrough?'

FitzHarding smiled. 'I thought you knew. I'm married to a kinswoman of his, and it was I who arranged for Dermot to send those ships to Henry's aid in the first place.'

Aha. I wasn't good at politics, but I saw that Robert FitzHarding was very good indeed.

Speaking slowly, weighing each word before I spoke, I said, 'If King Henry agrees to give Dermot Mac Murrough an army, I am willing to be part of that army. Provided, of course, that our king gives me his permission to do so. His formal permission.'

FitzHarding and I locked eyes. He understood what I meant. If I had the king's formal official permission, it would look as if I was in Henry's favour again. It would improve my own position very much. People would begin to think I might regain the earldom of Pembroke.

And so I might, if I was successful in this venture.

But one thing still bothered me. 'If Dermot Mac Murrough has had everything taken from him, how can he pay to hire a new army?'

'He has gold left,' FitzHarding assured me. 'He's no fool, he held onto his personal possessions and fortune. Besides, he's willing to give some of his kingdom, and other considerations, to any man who will help him regain his title.'

Some of his kingdom? *Land?* I drew in my breath sharply. Land was property. Land was power.

'I'm very interested indeed,' I told my friend. 'Keep me informed.'

'I shall,' he promised.

Robert FitzHarding was always as good as his word – which may have been why he had powerful friends. I had not been back at my castle for long before the first messenger arrived.

'Dermot Mac Murrough has followed King Henry to France,' I was told.

My spirits sank. If Henry had gone to France, that meant he would be very involved in other matters. He had taken a wife, a French woman called Eleanor, and hoped someday to rule both kingdoms. If Dermot appeared at his elbow, chattering about Ireland, Henry might be annoyed. Ireland would not seem very important to him compared to his own dreams. He might well refuse to have anything to do with Dermot Mac Murrough. He could forget the debt he owed – or more likely, he would simply refuse to honour it. Mac Murrough would have to go back to Ireland with his tail between his legs, a king who had lost his kingdom. And I would remain in England, an earl who had lost his earldom.

It was a bleak prospect. But I really did not expect anything better. My life had never gone well, it seemed to me.

'Why do you spend so much time at the gates of the castle?' Basilia asked me.

'I'm waiting for a messenger,' I told her.

I had a long wait before the next messenger arrived from Fitz-Harding. When I saw his horse coming up the road, I almost ran to meet it before I recalled who I was. I must be calm and stern and dignified. So I stood where I was and waited for him to come up to me, and for my herald to announce him.

Then I took the messenger into the hall and waited still longer while the servants gave him food and drink.

When at last he had wiped the grease from his mouth onto his sleeve, I leaned towards him.

'You have word of Dermot Mac Murrough?'

'I have indeed,' the man assured me. 'He found King Henry in France after a long search, and, after a longer wait, he was finally allowed to see him. The Irishman gave his submission to our king, and pledged his loyalty. In return, he asked for an army.'

'Did Henry give it to him?' I asked eagerly.

Chapter 9

AOIFE

Promises of Help

My father took the loss of his kingship very hard. A lesser man might have gone mad. But Father's fine brain never stopped working. When his enemies had his back to the wall, he always thought of a way to outwit and defeat them.

On the day he departed for England to ask the help of King Henry, I threw my arms around him. 'May God be with you!' I said.

I refused to believe that God was angry with my father. God must know, as I did, that Dermot Mac Murrough was no monster.

But there is an old saying: 'Every ass likes to kick at a dead lion.' When Father no longer had the power of the kingship behind him, people began telling all sorts of lies about him. They even said he had once blinded one of his hostages, the way the new High King, Rory O'Connor, had blinded some of his.

It was a terrible lie and I was very angry with the people who told it to me. I never spoke to them again. I knew that kings sometimes put out the eyes of men they considered a threat to them, but I had never seen my father be cruel to anyone – not in front of me, anyway.

I hate it when people lie about him.

When Tiernan O'Rourke learned that Father had left Ireland, he was very angry. He wasn't satisfied with having taken the kingship from my father. He wanted still more revenge.

He attacked Ferns.

Father had worked so hard to rebuild it after the fire, but now his enemies took it apart stone by stone. They tore down timber walls and levelled earthen banks, and burned everything that would burn.

Our poor, beautiful Ferns, destroyed again!

Afterwards some people said Father had burned it himself before he left, to keep O'Rourke from capturing it, but that wasn't true. Father loved Ferns, and it was our home. His enemies destroyed it.

O'Rourke wanted to destroy us as well, since Father had gone beyond his reach. But my uncle, Father's younger brother Murrough, begged for mercy for us. He and Donal had been left in charge of the family in Father's absence, and I'm sure Murrough was doing what he thought was right.

I was angry with him, though. 'Father would never have begged for mercy from his enemies!' I shouted at my uncle.

'Would you rather be killed?'

'Let them try!' I cried. 'I'll kill two men for every one who lays hands on me!'

Murrough gave me a long look. 'I think you would,' he said.

'I assure you she would,' Donal told him.

But Murrough asked for mercy anyway, and the High King granted it. Our lives were spared. But my brother Enna was taken away as a hostage, to be held against Father's return.

Kinsfolk took us in. They were brave to do so, for being kind to any of Dermot's family could earn the wrath of Tiernan O'Rourke.

So I spent my first Christmas away from my father, living under a roof that wasn't ours, wondering what the future held. Our family was torn apart. Father off across the sea somewhere, and poor Enna a hostage many miles away, among our enemies.

In the chapel, I prayed long and hard with my head bowed over my clasped hands. 'Please, God. Please take care of my father.'

We learned that the High King had named my uncle Murrough as King of Leinster in Father's place. I suppose O'Connor thought Murrough would be grateful to him for sparing our lives, and would be loyal. But he didn't know what a tight-woven clan we were. When every other person's hand was raised against us, we drew together more than ever.

Murrough came to see us a few days after Christmas. 'I've learned that Dermot has followed the English king to France,' he told us. He brought us food and furs. His words brought us hope.

Then we waited. There was no more news of Father for many weeks. We didn't know if he had found Henry, or if he was dead or alive.

Then on an early spring day of radiant sunshine, when the air was laced with lark song, Dermot Mac Murrough returned to Leinster.

When I heard his name being shouted across the fields I ran faster than anyone, so I would be the first to see him. He came riding on a lathered chestnut horse, with a small band of men-at-arms following him. Men with foreign faces.

There was grey in Father's hair and new lines on his face, but his arms were as strong as ever. He slid from his horse and lifted me high into the air, and I was a woman by then, and sturdy.

'Success, Aoife!' he cried. 'I've found warriors to follow my banner and I shall reclaim my kingdom! I finally caught up with Henry in France, where he spends much of his time. By marriage he is lord of the greater part of that land. He has agreed to help me. The King of England himself has agreed to help me!' He gave me a squeeze that took my breath away, and swung me around in the air.

At first it was enough to be in his arms again, with my nostrils full of the smells of sweat and leather and iron. But when he put me down at last I looked beyond him, to the foreigners with their strangely-coloured shields and unfamiliar armour. There were not very many of them.

'Is that your army, Father? Is that all the help the English king would give you?'

He barked a hoarse laugh. 'Of course not, this is just a small sample of the force to come. Henry couldn't give me his own army, you see, because he's engaged in a struggle for power in France now and needs every man he has. But he gave me permission to recruit warriors for myself among his Norman knights in England and Wales and that's what I've been doing.'

I gazed at my father in admiration. 'How did you persuade King Henry to help you?'

He rubbed his jaw with his thumb, as he always did when he was about to teach me something. 'Knowledge is power, Aoife. And I had a valuable bit of knowledge. I knew that the Pope, Adrian, was an Englishman. And I knew that King Henry was an ambitious man. Henry had once asked Pope Adrian for permission to undertake the conquest of Ireland. The Pope had agreed, but then Henry became busy with other problems and never acted on the plan.

'But I knew Henry must still want Ireland. What king would not want a land as rich as this? So when at last I was granted an audience with Henry I swore to him my loyalty, which would give him a foothold in Ireland, if he would support me against my enemies.'

I raised my eyebrows in surprise. 'You offered your loyalty to a foreign king?'

Father merely shrugged. 'Rory O'Connor or Henry Plantagenet, one High King is very like another. All any of them want is tribute, and I would as soon pay Henry as Rory. In fact I would rather. The English High King has done me no harm.'

Father's words made sense to me. They always did.

'So were you able to recruit many warriors among the Norman

knights in England?' I wanted to know.

'I did indeed. Every knight has his followers, much like a small king, and several such bands will be coming to Ireland to fight in my name soon. They won't all come at once, but the first of them will arrive this very spring. And in due course they will be joined by the man I've engaged to lead them. Then let my enemies beware!'

'Who is this man?' I wanted to know.

'His name is Richard de Clare. But he's known as Strongbow.'

Strongbow.

I had never heard the name before, yet it sent a shiver up my spine.

Chapter 10

RICHARD

A Kingdom of My Own

After Dermot Mac Murrough gained Henry's permission to raise an army, he returned to Bristol once more and stayed with Robert Fitz-Harding. I was summoned to meet him there.

My first impression of the former King of Leinster was that he was the largest man I had ever seen. Very tall, very broad, with a voice made hoarse by constant yelling in battle, he would strike fear into your heart if you faced him with raised swords between you. In Robert FitzHarding's house, however, he was soft-spoken and polite.

He wanted something from me and I wanted something from him. We were very pleasant to one another.

'Like myself,' Dermot said to me, 'you've been robbed of a title and lands that were yours by right.'

'I have,' I agreed.

'I can offer you more land and a better title,' he said. 'Ireland is fat, with green grass and gold in the streams. Come help me win back my kingdom and you'll have a kingdom of your own there.'

We were facing one another across Robert FitzHarding's table. Now I leaned back on my bench, folded my arms, and looked at Dermot through slitted eyes. I wanted him to know I wasn't easily fooled.

'I had one of the most powerful titles in this land,' I said. 'Earl of Pembroke. What can you give me that would be better? And what lands can you offer me, when your own kingdom has been taken from you?'

Dermot had expected my questions. 'When Leinster is mine again we needn't stop there. With a strong enough Norman force behind me I could challenge O'Connor himself, and become high king. Then I would have limitless land to offer you.'

'Perhaps,' I replied. 'But that's a dream. What can you give me now that's solid?'

'Even if we only win back Leinster I can give you a larger part of it than ever your family held in Wales,' Dermot assured me.

I scratched my head. I didn't know how large Ireland was, only scholars knew such things. And I had no idea how much land there might be in the province called Leinster. Dermot's words were tempting, but still he wasn't offering me anything I could count on. I would need a powerful reason to gather men-at-arms, leave my own land, and risk dying on foreign soil, fighting in what might well be a lost cause.

Dermot saw my hesitation. A gleam came into his eyes. 'I can offer you something else as well,' he said. 'Something that's in my power to give you this very minute. You're a widower, I believe?'

'I am.'

'I have a daughter called Aoife, who is as strong as a stone and as merry as a bird. There's no woman her equal in England, Wales, or Scotland. Come to Ireland and fight for me, and she is yours, to be your wife and bear your sons.'

As merry as a bird? I gave him a hard look, but there was no lie on his face. He was telling the truth about her, I would have sworn to it.

'She's young, this Aoife? And healthy?'

'Both in full measure,' Dermot assured me. 'And she's a king's daughter, a princess. How long has it been since one of your family married a princess?' he asked shrewdly.

I was dazzled, I admit it. Even my father would have been proud of me, if I married a king's daughter.

First, of course, we would have to make Dermot a king again.

I turned to Robert FitzHarding. 'Do we have King Henry's official permission for me to be involved in this venture?'

Robert drew a letter from his bosom. 'This is signed by the king himself,' he said. 'I shall read it to you.'

A flicker of contempt crossed Dermot's face. He looked at Richard. 'You cannot read? A Norman knight cannot read? Here, give it to me.' He snatched the letter from FitzHarding.

In a day of surprises, nothing surprised me more than discovering that the Irishman could read as well as any scholar!

'The letter reads thus,' he said, his eyes quickly scanning lines he must surely have read many times before. 'Henry, King of England, Duke of Normandy and Aquitaine, to all his men and to all nations subject to his sway, greeting. Whenever these letters come unto you, know that we have received Dermot, Prince of Leinster, into our grace and favour. Wherefore, whoever shall be willing to give him aid in recovering his kingdom, shall be assured of our favour.'

Assured of our favour. Assured of Henry's favour. I drew a deep breath. I would be happier if my name were mentioned, but this would do. It would have to do.

But I must be careful. I must drive as hard a bargain as I could, for I knew that no opportunity such as this would come to me again. I was admired for my strength, not my brains, yet on this one occasion I used my brains.

I pretended I still was not willing. I cleared my throat several times. I shuffled my feet. I got up and paced the room, pausing to gaze out the deep-set window towards the quays.

'Mmmm,' I said.

Out of the corner of my eye I watched FitzHarding and Mac Murrough. Both thought I would have agreed by now.

But they were asking a lot of me. If they wanted my help, they had to pay. And I wasn't going to agree until I was certain I had run the price as high as it would go.

Of course, Dermot Mac Murrough might lose his temper and walk out at any moment. I knew that. But I would be no worse off if he did.

So I waited.

At last I heard him push his bench back, stand up, and walk across the flagstoned floor towards me. He didn't touch me, but he stood close behind me, gazing out the same window.

'You're a clever man, de Clare,' he said. 'I like that. I'm sometimes reckless, myself, so I admire a man who takes time to think.'

I said nothing.

'I offer you land and an exceptional wife,' Dermot said.

'You do.' I continued to look out the window. Gulls were wheeling through the sky, dropping to earth to fight over scraps.

Dermot drew a deep breath. 'Robert FitzHarding tells me you're a fine warrior, the ideal man to lead this invasion. For such a man, there must be a special … reward.'

My heart began hammering in my chest. I didn't know what he was going to offer me, but I knew from the tone of his voice and the look on his face that it would be very valuable. I knew I was beginning to win, after a lifetime of having fortune go against me.

'Come to Ireland and fight for me,' said Dermot Mac Murrough, 'and restore me to my kingship, and when I'm dead it shall be yours.'

I stared at him. 'What are you saying?'

'Am I not clear? Make me King of Leinster again, and I say you will be King of Leinster after me.'

The room was so quiet, both Dermot and Robert heard me swallowing hard. This was beyond anything I had imagined.

A kingdom. The Irish man was offering me a kingdom!

King Richard.

A land of my own and a title beyond my wildest dreams!

A huge bubble swelled in my chest. I felt as if I was going to burst.

At the time, it didn't occur to me to ask Dermot if he had the right under Irish law to pass his title on to a man of his choice. Robert never thought of it either.

'You offer too much to resist,' I said to Dermot Mac Murrough. 'If we can agree on the details, I'm your man.'

He smiled at me then, and I smiled back. Only when I saw him smiling did I realise what sad eyes Dermot had.

Probably mine were just as sad. Except on this day.

Robert FitzHarding sent for fine French wine with which to toast our venture. Then Dermot and I got down to the hard business of settling the details. How many men he would need, how many weapons, how many horses. The horses were very important. He felt that even a small amount of cavalry could do great damage to the native warriors, who usually fought on foot.

It would take me some time to gather the army he wanted, I told him. I didn't explain just how little real power I had, or how hard it would be for me to recruit enough men. I simply said it would take time.

He wasn't pleased to hear this. Dermot Mac Murrough was a man who wanted everything done right away. There was a hard, shrewd brain behind those sad eyes, and he tried to force me to agree to things

I knew I couldn't do. But I held my ground and Robert FitzHarding supported me, and in the end the deal was done.

I left Bristol with my heart singing in me, to prepare for Ireland.

Chapter 11
AOIFE

Terrible News

I hated my father's enemies as much as he did. If I could have done, I would have beaten O'Connor and O'Rourke and their allies with my fists. I would have hurled stones at them and run spears through them.

Since I couldn't, I was glad Father had found men who would.

The one called Strongbow was not the only Norman who had sold his sword to us, though Father said he was the most important. He explained this to his two families, gathered in the borrowed house that was our home until he became king again, and could reclaim Ferns.

'This Strongbow held noble titles in England and is a very experienced warrior,' Father told us. 'He's a man who hates to lose as much as I do, which is one of the things I like about him. If I'm any judge of men, he's cold enough and hard enough and hungry enough to do just what I need.

'While waiting for him to gather the men he needs, I didn't sit idle, however. At the suggestion of FitzHarding I went deep into the heart of Wales, and found other willing warriors, including a man called FitzStephen, who was imprisoned in a dungeon with no prospects at all. I arranged for his release, so he owes me a debt.

'FitzStephen has followers of his own, as does a man called Maurice FitzGerald, whom I also spoke to. The two of them, like

Strongbow, are going to fight for me. In fact, they'll be arriving in Ireland soon, even before Strongbow.'

'Aside from getting FitzStephen out of prison, what rewards have you offered these men?' asked Donal Mac Murrough Kavanaugh.

Father's eyes twinkled. 'I've promised FitzStephen and FitzGerald the town of Wexford,' he said.

Wexford! We howled with laughter.

Wiping away the tears of mirth that were streaming from his eyes, Donal said, 'There's no man as clever as you! Wexford belongs to the Norse – you'll be giving away something that isn't even yours to give!'

Father chuckled too. 'Of course. Why should I give something of my own, something valuable to me, to some man I took out of a dungeon? When FitzStephen arrives the Norse will stand against him, as they're loyal to the High King at the moment. If he defeats them he helps defeat my enemies, so he's welcome to the marshes and bogs of Wexford. I've no liking for them anyway.'

We laughed again, but Donal, who had a head on him, had not finished asking questions. 'You didn't take the man called Strongbow out of a dungeon,' he pointed out. 'You said he had noble titles. What have you offered him? Surely something better than marshland and bogland.'

Father's senior wife jumped to her feet. 'Not my jewels!' cried Mor.

'Of course not. Those are your own property under the law. How could I give them away?'

'You're giving away Wexford,' I said, which set us all to laughing even harder.

Just then a messenger arrived. He was a barefoot boy with streaks of dirt on his face. His saffron-coloured tunic was torn as if he had run through briars. His face was pale.

'I seek Dermot Mac Murrough,' the lad said.

Father scraped back his bench and stood up. 'You have found him.'

The boy approached him very slowly, as if an unseen hand was pushing him from behind. He looked as if he was afraid of Father. What had he been told about Dermot Mac Murrough to frighten him so? Stammering, he managed to say, 'I b…bring word of your son, the one called Enna. He has been b…b…blinded by those holding him hostage.'

Father's face went white as milk. Mother gasped. Her eyes rolled back in her head. I caught her in my arms, but over her head I kept my eyes on Father. He stood unmoving as a standing stone.

Enna's eyes could not be restored. Enna's sight was gone forever.

Tears burned in my throat like fire, like hate.

I remembered Enna's blue eyes dancing as he taught me the song about the blue cow. Being ill so often had forced him to study more than the rest of us did, and he had become a fine scholar. Then he had begun to outgrow his illness, to become strong as well as wise. He might have made a king, someday.

Blinded, mutilated, he could never be a king. It was against the law. Enna must spend his life being cared for by others. Helpless. Humiliated. Just because he was his father's son!

I had never seen my father stand as tall, or look as fierce, as he did that day with his grief upon him. For the first time I understood why others might be afraid of him. When he spoke, his hoarse voice echoed from the rafters below the thatch.

'They have blinded my son,' he said. 'They have insulted my blood, denied my kingship … and ruined Enna's life. O'Rourke, O'Connor and their allies have reached into the heart of my family to do their terrible work. They didn't do this to me, but to one of my children. To one of my children!'

His voice rose to a shriek of fury. 'You asked what I offered to Strongbow? I shall tell you. To the man who destroys my enemies I would give anything. Anything!' He raised his clenched fists above his head with a sob of pure agony.

The pain ran through all of us. For a moment, I felt as if it was my own eyes that had been put out.

Much, much later, Father sought me out. He came to the chamber where I was caring for Mother, and asked me to walk with him.

Together we paced across the fields. The leaves would soon burst into glorious green and the sun was shining on our bare heads, but we couldn't feel its warmth. I knew we both felt the same inside. Cold and angry and bitter.

At last Father said, 'Would you be willing to do anything I asked of you, Aoife?'

'I would of course. Anything!'

'Don't be so quick to make that promise, even to me,' Father warned. 'Promises can be ... dangerous.'

'You wouldn't make me do anything dangerous.'

'I cannot make you do this at all. Under our law, you must be willing to marry the man. No one can force you.'

I stopped in my tracks. 'Marry?'

'Marry. Richard de Clare.'

Suddenly I understood. Donal had asked Father what he had promised Strongbow.

'You offered *me* as a reward!' I accused.

Father would not meet my eyes.

'You had no right,' I said. 'Under the law I'm a free person. You taught me that yourself.'

'I had no right,' he agreed in a soft, sad voice, nodding his greying head. 'But when Strongbow arrives in Ireland and sees how many enemies I have, and how strong they are, he may regret coming. I had

68

to offer him something valuable enough to make him willing to stay. And you're more valuable to me than anything else, Aoife.

'Will you do it for me? Will you marry Strongbow, for me?'

My head was spinning. I was of an age to marry, I had survived sixteen winters. But I didn't think about marriage all that often. Unlike my sisters, I had other interests.

Yet how could I refuse Father? He was asking something very important of me, something that only I could do for him.

Besides, I would marry someone. Sometime. Why not a Norman knight who was a great warrior?

'Tell me about Strongbow,' I said.

I could hear the relief in Father's voice. 'He's a man of almost my own age, Aoife, but still very strong, very powerful. Tall, with long arms. Skilled with the bow. Yet he's most courteous in his manner, almost gentle. It must come from his French background, his Norman blood.'

He didn't sound too bad, this Strongbow. My father's age, rather than some bold young lad, but I didn't mind about that. I loved my father, I could love a husband of his years as easily.

Still, there was something about that name. 'The first time I heard you say "Strongbow",' I told Father, 'I felt a chill on my heart.'

'It is a name to cause fear,' he agreed. 'And what's wrong with that? I want to strike fear into my enemies. But I promise you, Aoife, you need not fear the man. He'll make you a fine husband, there's noble blood in him. And I'll see to it that the two of you want for nothing.'

'Has he any wives across the sea?'

Father was too sad to laugh, but the corner of his lip curved upward just a little. 'The Normans only take one wife at a time,' he told me, 'and Richard de Clare is a widower.'

'So I'll be his senior wife, if I accept him?'

'His only wife, according to Norman custom.'

'What if he doesn't want me once he sees me?'

Now Father did laugh in spite of himself. 'Oh Aoife, Aoife!'

I was Father's favourite, and he thought any man would prize me. But I wasn't so sure.

Silently, I promised myself that when I met this Strongbow I would have stones in my plaits, and if he didn't like me I would hit him. If he tried to refuse me and go against Father's wishes, I would hit him terribly hard!

Chapter 12

RICHARD

Gathering Fighting Men

While I travelled the countryside gathering fighting men who were willing to sell their swords to Dermot Mac Murrough, Robert Fitz-Harding followed events in Ireland. Ships putting into Bristol brought frequent news across the Irish Sea to him. From time to time he sent messengers to me.

One messenger caught up with me when I returned to the castle to resupply. He gave me a lot to think about. When we had fed him a meal and sent him on his way, I went to talk to Basilia.

Talking to Basilia was always good for me. I could see things more clearly in my mind when I explained them to her.

We sat together on a stone bench in the courtyard, enjoying a rare ray of sunshine. The season had been cold and grey.

'Tell me about the Irish king,' Basilia said eagerly. She loved to hear tales from across the sea. They weren't real to her, she listened as if they were only stories. But she enjoyed them, even if she didn't understand that they were about real life-and-death matters.

'Dermot of Leinster has gone into hiding,' I told her. 'He doesn't want his enemies to know he's back in Ireland. He's keeping his head down in an Augustinian monastery in Ferns. Meanwhile, his brother Murrough – whom the Irish High King named as King of Leinster – is

71

rebuilding Dermot's old palace. I suspect he's not doing it for himself, but for Dermot. Dermot will surely expect to live in it again, just as he intends to be King of Leinster again.'

'He must be a brave man,' Basilia said. 'But not as brave as my brother, of course.' She smiled at me.

I smiled back. 'He'll need to be brave. The Irish High King and his friend, O'Rourke, have learned that Dermot is back. It couldn't long be kept a secret. They know he's brought a few warriors with him from England, and the High King thinks that Murrough has betrayed him for Dermot's sake. Which is probably true.

'So, I understand, O'Connor and O'Rourke are hastily gathering an army to teach Dermot a lesson.'

Basilia's eyes were as round as bowls. 'Oooo! Will they kill him?' To her it was only an exciting tale.

She could hardly wait until the next messenger arrived with more news from Ireland. Then I was able to tell her, 'Though he wasn't prepared for battle, Dermot Mac Murrough went out bravely to face O'Connor and O'Rourke. To buy time for his allies to arrive, he pretended he had no heart for war. He has agreed to a treaty that will allow him to retire in peace on a tiny scrap of the land he once ruled, and die an old man in his bed.'

Basilia looked disappointed. It wasn't a brave ending for the story.

'Don't worry, little sister,' I assured her. 'Neither Robert Fitz-Harding nor I think Dermot intends to keep the treaty and die in his bed. That wouldn't be like him.'

'What are the Irish like?' she wanted to know.

'Big, if Dermot Mac Murrough is anything to judge by. When I met him I was impressed with his size and strength. And the Irish customs and manners are very different from ours. The King of Leinster speaks good Church Latin, so I could talk to him, but his native tongue is as wild as Welsh.'

Basilia giggled. 'I hope you didn't say that to him.'

'Of course not,' I assured her. I was never diplomatic, I had no gift for saying careful things. But I had been careful for once in my life when I bargained with Dermot Mac Murrough.

There was an edge to the man that told me I must be careful in dealing with him. But I didn't say this to Basilia. I protected Basilia, always.

O'Connor was generous to the defeated Dermot. It does him credit. Dermot made the most of the truce the High King offered him, by very tardily paying the honour price for O'Rourke's stolen wife. He also swore loyalty to O'Connor.

I don't think he meant either gesture. In fact, I'm certain of it. Within weeks he was urgently demanding that his hired warriors set sail for Ireland at once. Messengers came to me at the gallop from Robert FitzHarding.

I wonder where Dermot got the hundred ounces of gold for the stolen wife's honour price. Later I heard a rumour that he had melted down his own wives' jewellery, but that may have been a spiteful lie. People said all sorts of things about Dermot Mac Murrough.

I didn't say any of this to Basilia, either. Like our mother, she wanted her life to be filled with flowers. She wanted to hear pretty stories about noble kings and queens.

My lovely little sister! Could I ever give her the kind of life I wanted her to have?

Word reached me that FitzStephen was preparing to depart for Ireland at the end of April, in the Year of Our Lord 1169. He had three ships and would take ninety horsemen and three hundred men-at-arms to Dermot Mac Murrough. An uncle of mine, Hervey de Montmorency, was going to go with him.

I summoned my captain, Raymond le Gros, and told him the news. 'I'm worried that these adventurers will claim the lands that are promised to me,' I said. 'So I've asked my uncle to be my eyes and ears in Ireland until we arrive.'

'How much of that promised land is going to be mine?' Raymond wanted to know.

Since I didn't know how much land there was, I could hardly give him a figure. 'All you earn,' I said.

'And your sister? If I have land, I want a wife.'

I sighed. I had very little to pay him with, and I needed him. It looked as if I might have to give Basilia to him. But if so, I must make him as wealthy as I could first. In the meantime he must wait. 'We'll talk about marriage after the invasion,' I told him. 'When you have property in Ireland.'

'When will that be?'

'It's taking a long time to recruit the size of army Dermot needs. Don't be so impatient, Raymond.'

But no one was as impatient as Dermot Mac Murrough. Every ship that crossed the Irish Sea brought fresh pleas from him, for men, for weapons. For an army, with me at its head.

Two more ships, led by other land-hungry Normans, set out for Ireland with ten horses and more men-at-arms.

As I would learn later, Dermot's son Donal Mac Murrough Kavanaugh met them. Forming an army with FitzStephen's men, they marched on the town of Wexford.

I didn't mind their attacking Wexford. I already knew that Dermot had promised it to FitzStephen and FitzGerald. A greater prize would be mine.

The people of Wexford must have been horrified to see an army of foreign warriors marching towards them, under not only Dermot's banner but also Norman banners. Knights on horseback were an unfamiliar sight, and the weapons they carried struck fear into the Wexford men.

The battle was savage, and after only two days, with the town blazing, the bishops came out and offered to surrender. Hostages were taken and the fighting ended.

'We've won our first battle,' I told Raymond le Gros when I heard the news. Hervey de Montmorency had sent me a glowing report by the first trading vessel out of Wexford afterwards.

'We marched on to Ferns,' my uncle informed me, 'to the royal stronghold of Dermot Mac Murrough. His palace there is rebuilt and he has taken control of it once more. From there, we attacked the tribe who had blinded his son, Enna. They're allies of the High King, and thought they'd win his favour by blinding Enna, but they regret their folly now. We made them pay dearly for it.'

I am sure they did. Dermot Mac Murrough would have taken a terrible revenge for his son's eyes.

Meanwhile, I was slowly putting together the main army of invasion. I wanted mounted knights, foot soldiers, and, in spite of the Church, plenty of archers. I trusted the bow and arrow.

News of that first victory at Wexford was helping me recruit soldiers. 'There will be land for all of you,' I promised. 'Dermot of Leinster has already given Wexford town and the land around it to the first men to fight for him, but Ireland is vast and there will be plenty for each of you. Plenty.'

I hoped I was right. But the one thing I really wanted was to be certain there would be land for me. Never again would I be a landless lord!

Chapter 13
AOIFE

A King's Daughter

When FitzStephen and the other Anglo-Normans reached Ferns, we jostled one another for a look at them. My first impression was that they walked like strangers in a strange land, with their feet wide apart, their arms at the ready, and their shoulders rounded against blows.

Father welcomed FitzStephen and his half-brother, a man called FitzGerald, into our hall, together with one Hervey de Montmorency. 'He's the uncle of Strongbow,' Donal said to me behind his hand.

I wasn't impressed by Hervey de Montmorency.

He was tall, but not so tall as Father. He had grey eyes that bulged from his head. His waist was narrow but he had a round belly, and he jabbered away in a language I didn't know, waving his hands quite wildly as he talked.

When he spoke to Father, however, he changed to a halting sort of Latin. Then I could understand what he said. Father saw me trying to listen, and beckoned me to come forward.

'This is my daughter Aoife,' he told de Montmorency.

Strongbow's uncle looked me up and down the way Father would look at a horse he was thinking of buying. 'Has she all her teeth?'

I answered by baring them at him.

He raised his eyebrows. 'Does she understand Latin?'

'Aoife is educated,' Father said proudly. 'She's a king's daughter.'

The Norman looked shocked. 'You Irish educate women? Whatever for?'

Father told him, 'Noble women have that right, under our law.'

'Women have no rights. They're property.'

Now it was Father's turn to look shocked. 'You're speaking of my daughter!'

'And you've sold her to my nephew Richard. She's property,' de Montmorency insisted.

I doubled my fists. I was very angry. 'No one sold me!' I blurted out. 'And if I don't like this nephew of yours I'll have nothing to do with him. I'll spit in his face. I'll kick his shins. I'm not property, I am Red Eva!'

I tossed my head and stalked away. I could feel the Norman's eyes on me.

'You Irish are savages,' I heard him say in astonishment. I don't think my father liked him very much after that.

But we had to be nice to these foreigners. They had come to Ireland to help us, after all. Without them, Father's enemies would have destroyed us.

As it was, they dumped poor blinded Enna at the border of our land like a sheep sent to market, with his hands and feet tied tight with leather thongs, and his poor empty eye sockets gaping.

He was alive, but no more than that.

I sat beside him in his chamber and bathed his wounds. The sweetest holy water would not make him see again, nor restore the life he could have had. My tears mingled with the water I used on his face.

'Aoife?'

'What is it, Enna?'

'Are you crying?'

77

His hearing seemed to be sharper, now that he couldn't see. I rubbed my eyes with my fist. 'I never cry.'

'I can never cry again,' my brother replied.

I promised myself then, that if Strongbow destroyed my father's enemies I would marry him and be a good wife to him, even if he had bulging eyes and a fat belly.

But when was he coming to Ireland?

That question was on everyone's tongue. At Ferns we spoke of little else as the year wore away and one battle followed another.

Father's hired warriors were good fighting men. They won more than they lost, and Father brought back many cattle and much loot from the chieftains they defeated.

But the Anglo-Normans hadn't come to Ireland for cattle. They wanted land. Wexford wasn't enough for them. They asked for more and more. Father gave bits and strips, but they were never satisfied.

Then we received bad news indeed. 'The High King is preparing a great hosting with many warriors,' a messenger announced to my father. 'O'Connor is bringing together the largest army seen in Ireland for many years. He means to break your back, if you resist him.

'But he's a generous king, and offers you one chance to avoid your own destruction. Turn against the foreigners you've brought into this land, and the High King won't attack you.'

Father was furious. 'Tell the High King that these men came to Ireland at my request, and I won't betray them now. What sort of man does he think I am?'

But the Normans didn't like the sound of the army the High King was gathering. Some of them came to Father with a suggestion of their own. 'Winter is coming,' they reminded him, 'and winter is a bad season for war. The ice and mud make fighting very hard. We think we should go home for the winter, and return to you in the spring.'

He tried to argue with them, but they wouldn't listen. They didn't all leave. FitzStephen, who was now master of Wexford, was glad enough to stay and enjoy his new wealth, and some others stayed with him.

But Father's forces were seriously reduced.

'What will you do now?' Donal asked him.

'Perhaps I'll make peace with O'Connor,' Father said with a twinkle in his eye. 'Just for a while. Just until Strongbow arrives.'

'Do you still think he's coming?' I wanted to know.

'I'm certain he is. I have the man's word, and if I read him rightly, he's not one to lie,' Father assured me.

Later that same day, however, I was crossing the courtyard just in time to see a messenger set out on a fast Kildare horse. When I asked at the stable, I was told he was heading for the coast, with a message from Father to be sent to Strongbow on the next ship to England.

Come to me, Father was urging the Norman. Come as soon as you can. Don't forget your promise.

The harvest was gathered, a fine heavy harvest as it always was when my father was King of Leinster. Then the nights drew in, long and cold and dark, and winter was upon us. Men sat huddled around the hearth, talking about the battles of the past and the battles to come. Talking of Strongbow, and the victory he would one day win over O'Connor and O'Rourke.

Mor and Sive talked mostly about Dervorgilla. 'The blame for all our troubles lies at her feet,' they told each other. 'She urged Dermot to take her away from her cruel husband, and stealing her was the worst thing he ever did. It cost him a kingdom and could cost him his life one day. It's all the fault of Dervorgilla!'

I had never met the woman, but I wasn't certain they were right. It was hard to imagine anyone talking Father into doing something he didn't want to do. He had wanted to steal Dervorgilla to get even with

Tiernan O'Rourke, just as much as she had wanted to get away from the man.

I watched Dermot's two wives as they sat close to the fire, being company for one another, gossiping with their heads together. They could talk talk talk all day long, and they said the same things to each other over and over again. I don't want to be like them, I thought. But what sort of life would I have?

Ships carried the hired warriors back across the Irish Sea until Father's army was a shadow of what it had been. If he was worried, he didn't let us see his fears. Instead he seemed much as he always had been, strong and confident.

'Strongbow will come in the new year,' he told us many times. 'You'll see. He'll bring an army to put fear into the High King himself. We've only to wait. The final victory will be ours.'

And so we waited, through the dark and dreary winter, filling our days with talk and our nights with worry. But Father did more than simply wait, of course.

Chapter 14
RICHARD

Facing King Henry II

The last boatload of adventurers to return from Ireland brought interesting news indeed. Dermot Mac Murrough had made a treaty with Rory O'Connor. In return for being allowed freedom of action in Leinster, he had formally accepted O'Connor as High King of Ireland and paid tribute to him.

'He must have done it with gritted teeth,' I said to Raymond le Gros.

'If Dermot has pledged his loyalty to the High King, does that mean he won't want us any longer?' asked Raymond.

I smiled grimly. 'Not at all. He's simply fighting for time. Why do you think he keeps sending me messages?'

'He'll break his pledge to the High King then, when we arrive?'

'I'm certain of it,' I told Raymond.

My captain frowned. 'If he would break a pledge to his High King, what makes you think he'll keep his promises to you?'

Now that was a question to cause me some worry!

Pacing the battlements of my castle, I thought about Dermot Mac Murrough. What sort of man was he, really? There were so many tales told of him. I sent for my uncle, Hervey de Montmorency, who had recently returned from Ireland.

Over bowls of wine, into which we dipped great hunks of black bread, I asked my uncle for his opinion of the King of Leinster.

'He's as slippery as a buttered fish. You met him, Richard. What was your opinion of him?'

'Much the same,' I admitted. 'Yet I found him cheerful in spite of his misfortune, a quality I much admire.'

My uncle told me, 'He's devoted to his family, also. I've never seen any man dote on his children as does Dermot mac Murrough.'

Ah, then. That was a relief to my mind. If Dermot was so fond of his children, he wouldn't want to anger his daughter's husband. He would keep his promises to me, I felt. Once I owned his daughter I would be in a strong position with him.

At the time I met my uncle, I had only two servants to wait on me at table, and one of them was borrowed from the dairy for the occasion. They were poor shabby creatures with hungry eyes, and as I talked to Hervey I tried to keep watching them. Either would steal a bit of our food if they could.

Peasants. I wondered that some people claimed they had souls, like Christians.

My uncle scratched his chest and turned on his bench, hoping for more wine. 'By the bye, Richard, what's taking you so long, gathering this army you've promised Dermot Mac Murrough?'

I wanted more wine myself. 'Much of my strength was lost when the earldom of Pembroke was taken from me,' I reminded him. 'Men aren't eager to follow the banner of a knight who has lost his honours. I'm having to win them almost one man at a time, through threats or promises, and it's not easy. We need not only men, but horses and weapons and armour. It's a huge undertaking. I keep delaying my departure and making excuses to Dermot which I'm certain he doesn't like. But I dare not go to Ireland until I'm ready and can be certain of some success.'

There was so much to be won. It would be so easy to lose every-thing, if I made a mistake.

I couldn't talk of this to Basilia. I didn't want her to worry. Her fu-ture as well as mine hung in the balance.

I paced the battlements of the castle, gazing out in the direction of Ireland as if I could see that distant island. That unknown frontier. That strange, wild, dangerous place, where a fortune and a kingdom could be won. Or lost.

How does a man make himself step off into the unknown?

I went to see Robert FitzHarding. He was also beginning a new life. Age had forced him to give up his post as Portreeve of Bristol and he was about to enter the Augustinian order. This would be my last visit with him.

When we spoke of the planned invasion of Ireland, Robert made a wise suggestion. 'You should send an advance party before you go yourself, Richard. Have someone you trust learn just which way the wind is blowing. Many things have happened in Ireland, I'm sure, since FitzStephen and the others first went over.'

His advice was sound. But who could I send? Then I thought of my captain, Raymond le Gros.

'You're the man I would trust with such a mission,' I told him.

Raymond was flattered by my faith in him. 'You may rely on me,' he assured me. 'But if I'm going to take an advance party into a for-eign land and great danger, I want to be certain of my reward before I go.'

'You'll have part of whatever we win,' I told him.

'I want more than that. You know what I want. Your sister, Basilia. I want your firm promise to give her to me as wife before we leave for Ireland.'

I felt trapped. The more I tried to put Raymond off, the more deter-mined he became. At last he made an argument I couldn't resist. 'If you marry Basilia to someone here, she'll always be in England,' he said. 'But if you marry her to me, once we're in Ireland I'll send for her to join us.'

Although under the law she had no say in the matter. I spoke to Basilia. 'Raymond le Gros wants to marry you.'

'Which one is he? The tall fair man with the bright blue eyes?' she asked hopefully.

'Ah … not quite. He's shorter, and rather … fat,' I had to admit. 'But he's the captain of my guards and I mean to give him lands and a title once we're in Ireland.'

Basilia frowned. 'Fat.' She took a deep breath. Then she forced a smile that broke my heart. 'If that's what you want, Richard,' she said.

From that moment I was more determined than ever to do well in Ireland. I must make Raymond a nobleman worthy of my little sister.

I didn't worry so much about my children. They would stay in England. They had never been as close to me as Basilia, I'm sorry to say. It wasn't their fault; their mother had turned them against me when they were very young. I would always provide for them as best I could, but it wouldn't hurt half as much to leave them behind, as it would hurt to leave Basilia.

So I gave her to Raymond, to marry and bring to Ireland when we were established there. My heart burst at the sight of my little sister in her wedding robes. I pretended to have a cold, and blew my nose many times.

Then all at once Basilia was gone! She went to live with Raymond's family until he could give her a home in Ireland.

I felt that everything was slipping away from me. I needed to get some sort of control.

A couple of years had passed since Henry had written the letter that promised his favour to anyone who would help Dermot Mac

Murrough. I needed to be certain the offer still held.

Kings have a way of changing their minds.

What if I had given my sister away, then went to Ireland only to find Henry wouldn't support my venture? I would be stranded in a strange land, with my bridges burned. It was a frightening prospect for a lonely, middle-aged man.

Henry was in England, at least for a few months, so I decided to meet him face to face and ask his permission and his blessing. I wanted to assure him that I, Richard de Clare, would be the man who formally planted his flag in Ireland.

I didn't look forward to meeting him. He had a long memory. What if he threw me into a dungeon as soon as he saw me? He could. Kings had that right and no one could argue.

But I couldn't go on until I had his personal agreement. It was too uncertain and dangerous. In the dark of night, I tossed sleeplessly on my bed and wondered how I had got myself into such a situation.

My squire oiled and polished my armour. He saddled my biggest, most impressive horse, and I gathered my tallest, strongest men to be my escort. Then I set out, hiding my fears behind a stony face, for the court of King Henry.

Arriving in London town, I found lodgings for myself and my men at an inn beyond the walls. Then I sent word to the king. 'Strongbow is here!'

He kept me waiting for several days before replying. At last a messenger came to me, however, and said I was to be taken into the king's presence at the great, grim stronghold built by William of Normandy.

This would be the first time I had actually met Henry Plantagenet. I didn't know what to expect. What I found was a thick-set, red-faced man, with a round head and small, sharp eyes. He never seemed to sit down, but strode up and down the audience chamber the whole time I was there. His courtiers bustled after him. From time to time he gave one of them a shove, more out of sport than malice.

'Do I understand you plan to go to Ireland, de Clare?' he asked me in French. French was the first language of the Plantagenets.

'I do, Your Majesty. With your permission, of course.'

He paused in his striding, long enough to scowl at me. 'Did I give you permission?'

This was the delicate moment. He could deny having done so. He could even take it back. 'You gave Dermot Mac Murrough a letter promising your favour to whoever would help him,' I said carefully.

'Did I?' He began pacing again. Heavy gold chains around his neck clanked with every step. 'Perhaps I don't remember,' he said craftily.

'I'm certain Your Majesty forgets nothing,' some anxious courtier was quick to say. Henry glared at the man, who ducked his head and tried to make himself small.

'Everyone wants something from me,' Henry snapped. 'What do you want, de Clare?'

'To serve my king,' I said.

'And? You want something else, surely. What is it? Land?'

'I'm in need of land, Your Majesty,' I admitted.

'Everyone wants more land,' said the king shortly. He stalked past me. I thought he was dismissing me. Then at the last moment he half-turned, and said to me over his shoulder, 'You have my leave to seek your fortune under the Irish king, as far as your feet will bear you.'

With a laugh that had no warmth in it, he left the audience chamber. His attendants ran after him.

I stood alone in the echoing room. Henry had been playing with me. I knew it. But in jest he had said words to me that could be taken to mean what I wanted. And others had heard him say them.

It would have to be enough. I knew I would get no more. If I was successful in Ireland, and only then, I would petition him again. Then he might formally regrant the earldom of Pembroke to me.

At first light the next morning my men and I had our backs to London and were hurrying westward.

Chapter 15

AOIFE

Normans at Baginbun

My father had run out of patience, if he ever had any. He wrote a long letter to Strongbow.

'We have watched the storks and swallows,' he wrote, 'the summer birds have come and are gone with the wind of the south. But neither winds from the east nor the west have brought your much-desired presence.'

Father was pleased with this letter. There was poetry in it, and as every Irish person knew, poetry had power.

Even before Strongbow could have received the letter, its magic seemed to be at work, for his advance guard arrived. Word came to us of a ship that had landed on the strand of Baginbun, in Bannow Bay. The ship flew Norman banners, and brought ten knights and seventy archers, led by a man known as Raymond le Gros.

Hervey de Montmorency, Strongbow's uncle, who had returned to Ireland, went to meet him. Father sent word to his own warriors to gather and be ready, but they were scattered and it would take time for them to come together.

However, Father's enemies in Waterford and Ossory were not scattered. They were ready and willing to fight.

The first messenger to reach Ferns from the scene of the battle had a thrilling tale to tell. 'Our enemies numbered three thousand men!' he cried, with the light shining from his eyes. 'But Strongbow's captain, Raymond le Gros, wasn't easily frightened. He captured many cattle, then caused them to stampede into the enemy lines. There was a panic and the enemy broke and ran. Le Gros chased them, and he and his men caught over five hundred and put them to the sword.'

'I knew it!' Father cried with joy, beating his fist against his open palm. 'I knew the tide would turn for us! God's blessing on the Norman and his kind!'

'There was a bitter argument afterwards,' the messenger went on to say. 'Seventy of the principal men of Waterford were taken prisoner and held in our camp. Raymond le Gros thought they should be shown mercy. But Hervey de Montmorency said mercy never won wars. He insisted that their legs be broken, then had them thrown over the cliff into the sea.'

I gasped with horror. I hated Father's enemies, but no man should suffer such a fate. It was as bad as blinding Enna.

A shadow seemed to cross Father's face for a moment. But then he hid it. He ordered a great feast of celebration to be prepared, and had the priests say prayers for Raymond le Gros and for Strongbow, who was surely soon to follow.

We filled our bellies with roast boar and duck eggs and haunch of badger, and there was laughter once more at Ferns. But privately, I wondered if we were ever going to see this Strongbow.

After that first victory, Raymond le Gros fell quiet. He really had very few men, and had won through luck and inspiration. He didn't want to have to fight again until Strongbow arrived to add to his numbers. Even the warriors Father was able to send to him couldn't persuade him to leave his camp and set out against O'Connor and O'Rourke.

Father's first joy turned sour. 'These Normans always want to wait for something,' he complained. 'It's an ugly habit. They're too cautious. I thought they were eager warriors, but now I'm not so sure.'

The weeks dragged by. Nothing was happening. Father rode out to meet with le Gros and Strongbow's uncle a number of times, urging them to fight, but nothing came of it. Without their support he was unwilling to march.

In time it would be winter again, another year lost, and his hatred for his enemies as strong as ever. When it began to soften he had only to look at poor Enna, feeling his way around the palace with his hands.

Enna was the torch that kept all our hatred burning.

But where was Strongbow?

Chapter 16

RICHARD

I've Come to Be a King

Remembering Henry's words as if they were a solemn pledge of lands and power, I headed westward, gathering the last men I needed along the way. The summer was drawing to a close. If we meant to take a serious invasion force to Ireland in the year of Our Lord 1170, we must set sail soon.

I went to the holding that belonged to Raymond le Gros' family, to say goodbye to my sister. If all went well in Ireland, in time she would be living in a fine castle of her own rather than a small mean house with her husband's kin.

We didn't know what to say to each other. I couldn't ask her if she was happy. I couldn't tell, from the look on her face.

Then she smiled at me as she always had, and ran into my arms. 'Oh Richard, do be careful in Ireland!' she breathed in my ear. 'And take care of Raymond for me, will you?'

I knew she was happy, then. One small stone was lifted from my heart.

'I'll not only take care of him, I'm going to make him a very wealthy man,' I promised Basilia. I said it as firmly as I could, to make her believe it. To make myself believe it as I stepped off the rim of the world. 'There's a much better future waiting for all of us,' I said.

Somehow, I must make it so.

Trusting that Raymond had prepared the ground and had our allies waiting, I led my army to Milford Haven. From that port we would depart for Ireland as soon as the last supplies were loaded aboard our ships.

But no sooner did I reach Milford Haven than a messenger on a fast horse caught up with me. He brought word from King Henry.

My heart sank as I listened.

'His Majesty fears the Earl of Strigul has misunderstood him, or taken advantage of his good nature. The king demands that the Earl of Strigul disband his army and undertake no foreign conquest, under threat of losing his last earldom.'

I was shocked. Why had Henry changed his mind? Was he afraid of any other man who could put together an army? What sort of threat could I be to him?

And, once I thought about it, what sort of threat was this to me? He said he would take my last earldom from me. But the title Earl of Strigul was of little importance any more. In Ireland, I would have vast holdings and be a king.

A king.

I thought long and hard, in the silence of the night. By morning I had made up my mind. Calling my ship's captains together, I told them, 'Finish loading as soon as you can. We sail at once.'

I had done everything possible to win the king's favour. I had even made an extra effort to be certain of his permission.

Now he had turned his back on me. Very well. It wasn't the first time a man had turned his back on me. My own father had done so, but I had survived. I had grown strong.

When the tide turned, we sailed for Ireland.

Aboard ship I stood at the rail, watching the sea. The water rose and fell, heaving up slate-coloured mountains that sank back into hissing foam.

My belly began to heave too.

I bit the inside of my lip but it didn't help. I tried not looking at the water, but staring up at the sky. The heaving grew worse. Sweat broke out on my brow. Think of something else, I ordered myself. But I couldn't think of anything else. Ireland, Dermot, the king ... all faded away. I gripped the splintery wooden rail as hard as I could. My knuckles turned white. The ship swooped and swayed and suddenly I was leaning out over the rail, being terribly sick.

I thought all my insides were coming out of me.

When at last I stood up again, I was dizzy. My ears were ringing. But when I looked around, I saw that I wasn't the only one who was seasick. On both sides of me were strong, brave warriors, with green faces, hanging over the rail and moaning.

'I think I'll stay in Ireland forever,' I said to the man nearest to me. 'I never want to be on a ship again.'

He nodded in agreement. He was too sick to speak.

In truth, I might have to stay in Ireland no matter what happened. By ignoring the king's command I was guilty of treason. Unless I won great victories in Ireland and claimed the entire island for him, he might never allow me to return. Or if I did, he would have me killed.

It was not a pleasant prospect.

Looking beyond the ship on which I stood, I saw the other ships carrying the rest of the two hundred knights and the thousand men-at-arms I had gathered, plus horses and weapons and armour.

It had taken a long time, longer than I would have liked, but at last I had put together a real army.

Perhaps that's why Henry forbade me to go, I thought. Men loyal to him might have seen us marching through the country and sent word to him of the size of my forces. No king likes to hear that another man, who was once set against him, has raised an army.

How good it felt to know I had enough power to worry a king! My sickness began to leave me. I gazed at the sea and the sky. I licked my lips and tasted the salt on them.

I turned my face toward Ireland.

Waterford was my destination, to join the advance party under Raymond le Gros. Our ships would come ashore on the 23rd of August, with good fighting weather still remaining to us.

As we neared land, I stood in the prow, eager for my first sight of Ireland. The ship's captain came up to me.

'Almost there now. You see that low dark line on the horizon? Land, that is. We'll put in near a place called Passage, where the Barrow and the Suir rivers pour into the harbour.'

I leaned forward as if I would push the ship faster with my own weight.

As we drew near the harbour, I could see the fleet of trading vessels that dotted its waters. Beyond stretched a green land, a rich land. A sweet land, it seemed to my weary eyes. The sky was as clear as a nun's voice, and the wind was soft on my cheek. Never had I seen a place so beautiful. We had left England under grey skies. When we reached Ireland, the sun appeared.

'I want to be the first on shore,' I told the ship's captain. A hundred years earlier, William of Normandy had been the first man ashore on English soil, and he had taken that land as his own.

I didn't wait for the boat to be properly beached but leaped out as if I was a lad of fifteen. Until the day I die I'll remember the thud of my feet on Irish soil, and the tingle that ran through my body.

'I've come to be a king,' I said into the soft wind.

It took the better part of a day to get all my men and equipment ashore, and set up camp. Messengers from Raymond arrived almost at once. Many eyes had seen us come ashore. By the time the first fire was lit for the night, Raymond himself had joined me.

'You're most welcome to Ireland,' he said heartily, clapping me on the shoulder. 'I almost despaired of you.'

'I said I would come. I came.' There was nothing else to say.

He turned slowly, his eyes measuring the huge force encamped around me. 'This is an army indeed. I expected nothing like.'

'There was no point in doing it half-way,' I told him.

'And when do we begin?'

'At once.'

Now that I was in Ireland, my patience was gone like melted snow. I couldn't wait to claim the lures that had brought me. I sent word to Dermot Mac Murrough, but without waiting for him, decided to put the town of Waterford under siege and force its surrender.

'Waterford,' Raymond had told me, 'was badly shocked by the killing of its most important men. But they've kept guards on the walls of the town, and the gates are barred. It's the most important trading centre in Ireland, Richard, after Dublin, and its capture would make a mighty beginning for us.'

'I think we made a bad start, killing important men,' I said doubtfully. 'It would have been better to make allies of them.'

Raymond snorted. 'How can you make allies of these people? We've come to take their land for ourselves, they'll not love us for it. I wanted to show them mercy at first but the others talked me out of it, and now I think they're right. If we show these people mercy they'll think we're soft. We must be hard. We must frighten them from the beginning. Live up to the name of Strongbow!' he said with a laugh.

I sent for a messenger. I set my face in hard lines as I spoke to him, knowing he would report my expression to the King of Leinster.

'Tell Dermot Mac Murrough to bring his men and attend the capture of Waterford if he likes,' I said, 'but assure him I, Strongbow, can do it without him.'

I would. Raymond was right. The time had come for me to be Strongbow indeed.

We attacked the walls twice, and were twice turned back. Then Raymond came to me with a plan. 'I've noticed a small timber building fixed to one of the walls,' he said. 'It's an outpost for guards, I think. But the important thing is, it has been built into the wall. If it were torn loose, part of the wall would come with it.'

I was beginning to be glad I had given my sister to Raymond le Gros.

My men attacked the sentry post with a will, hacking at it with their weapons while the defenders hurled spears and curses at us from the walls of the town. Soon the little timber building came down, with a crash. When the dust had settled we could see that the wall was broken.

We poured through. I was in the forefront, yelling. Never have I felt so brave in battle, or so eager. Together with my men I hacked and slashed and killed until we reached the centre of the town, where a stone cathedral stood.

Only then did I recall that these people were Christians. My upraised arm trembled. I put down my sword and stood, panting. But my army didn't stop. They fought most savagely, until the two Norse chieftains of the town came and offered to surrender.

They were sent to me and knelt before me with bowed heads as if I were a king.

Around us, their town burned.

Chapter 17

AOIFE

Meeting a Future Husband

After so long a wait, once Strongbow reached Ireland things happened with dizzying speed. No sooner had we learned of his arrival than a messenger came from him, inviting Father to take part in the capture of Waterford.

My father was startled. He told me, 'I thought Strongbow would want to meet me first so we could plan together. I thought he'd want my advice, my ideas, my leadership …'

'He doesn't appear to need it,' I remarked thoughtlessly. It was the first time I ever recall hurting my father's feelings, and I was sorry at once.

Father went off by himself, with a black scowl on his face. He made no effort to hurry to Waterford. Nor, as it proved, was there any need. Within two days we learned that Waterford had fallen, and now Father was being formally summoned by the conqueror.

'Richard de Clare, Earl of Strigul, requests Dermot, King of Leinster, together with his daughter Aoife, to attend him at once in Waterford town,' the messenger announced.

Father was both furious and admiring at the same time. 'The man struts like a peacock!' he cried. 'How dare he all but order me to come? What arrogance.' Then he smiled. 'What a victory, Aoife.

Imagine. Two days in Ireland, and he has already taken Waterford. What can I not do with such a man on my side?'

My mother was terribly excited. 'You're going to meet the man you may marry,' she kept reminding me, 'and we want you to look your best.'

I tossed my head. 'Let him worry about looking his best for me. If I don't like him, I won't marry him.'

Mother sighed. 'You're still like a wild animal. I hope this Strongbow can tame you.'

But Father merely said, 'Don't shame me, Aoife.'

Then my feelings were hurt. I would never, ever, do anything to shame him! So I stood quietly and let them plait my hair and bathe my body and dress me in fine robes. Our stock of gold and silver ornaments was not as large as it had once been, but rings were found for my arms and fingers, and a band of gold was twisted around my throat. Then I was wrapped in a new wool cloak and Father with his own hands set me upon the second best horse he had.

Followed by his warriors, we rode for Waterford.

Even from a distance, we could see the dark spirals of smoke rising from the captured town. I remembered the day I had seen Ferns burning, and wondered if Father was thinking of that too. But when I looked at him his face was blank. He stared straight ahead.

The northern gateway of the city gaped open, for the big timber gates had been torn from their iron hinges and burned. It was like Ferns all over again, but worse. We could smell death on the warm August air.

As we rode through the gates, I saw the first pile of bodies. They lay everywhere in the laneways of the town. I couldn't help seeing them.

Until that day Father had tried to keep me safe from the sights and sounds and smells of battle. Now I saw it all. This was not a game and these people would never get up and walk away, laughing.

I shuddered. 'What have we brought into Ireland?' I asked Father. But he didn't answer.

The ways were so clogged with bodies we had to get down off our horses and walk. Soot drifted on the air. My fine clothing was soon black with it, and I could feel the weight of ash on my face.

Ahead of us we could hear men yelling. A woman came stumbling towards us, her clothes torn and her hair wild around her face. 'They've killed our chieftain!' she moaned. In her grief she didn't recognise us, but thought we were citizens of Waterford.

My father stopped and put a kindly hand on her shoulder. 'I'll say a prayer for him,' he said.

She looked at him with grateful tears in her eyes, then ran on.

Strongbow must be somewhere up ahead, where the yelling was.

Men in foreign armour were running in and out of houses, carrying loot. One of them started to speak to me but Father drew his sword, and gave the man such a black look he backed away.

On we went through the ruined town, picking our way among smouldering timbers and piles of rubble.

Then we saw a crowd gathered in front of the cathedral. A crude platform had been built there. Afterwards I learned it was where the invaders had executed one of the local chieftains. As we approached, several of the men in the crowd turned towards us.

All at once I was frightened. My heart began beating so hard I thought they could see it jumping inside my gown. I wasn't afraid of the strangers in their armour, or of the dead bodies on every side.

I was afraid of change.

I didn't want my life to change. Adventures were lovely, but I had always been able to go home at the end of the day to my own family and my own familiar place.

Strongbow would put an end to that. He would change everything.

My feet began to drag through the rubble and ash. Father gave me a sharp glance. 'Come, Aoife,' he said. 'There's no turning back.' I heard an echo of sadness in his voice that frightened me still more, but he caught hold of my arm and pulled me forward.

One of the men waiting for us was Hervey de Montmorency. He was talking to a taller man who had long arms and a short neck, a man wearing badly dented armour. As we drew near, de Montmorency said something to this man, then pointed right at me.

I didn't need anyone to tell me that the man in the battered armour was –

'Strongbow!' cried my father, hurrying forward.

Strongbow was not what I expected. In my mind, a man with that name should have been a splendid giant, more mighty than anyone, with lightning flashing from his eyes. A warrior like Cuchulain, who could freeze his enemies' blood with a glance.

Richard de Clare wasn't like that at all. He was just a man, almost as old as my father, a tired-looking man with grime on his face. He had taken off his iron helmet and held it cradled in one arm. His hair was sandy-red, and thinning. When he spoke his voice was almost as high as a woman's.

'I see you've brought one of my rewards,' he said to Father. Then he looked into my eyes, and smiled as if pleasantly surprised.

Chapter 18
RICHARD

A Strange Irish Custom

Waterford town had been bravely defended by its people. Fear made them fight even harder. They were afraid of us because of what my uncle had done to their most important men. It had been a brutal act, and when I learned of it I wasn't pleased. I don't think it's wise policy in time of war to make people hate you too much. That can make peace impossible, later.

My uncle and I argued over it, and over the fate of the two chieftains of the town. At last we had come to an agreement. One was executed, to satisfy Hervey de Montmorency and those who thought like him, and the other was spared to balance the scales. I wanted these strangers to know that I could show mercy.

Waterford was ours. The first step was taken, there was no going back.

Dermot Mac Murrough arrived with the first of my rewards, the one that would assure me of the others. 'Strongbow!' he called as he came striding towards me through the ruined town.

Beside him was a very young woman, with heavy red hair and Dermot's own wilful expression. She was surely the daughter he had promised me as a wife. I liked the look of her. Her mouth was shaped for laughing.

She was not laughing now, however. She didn't look happy, she looked more like a shy child. For a moment she put me in mind of my sister Basilia, though they were not in any way alike.

I smiled at her gently, as I would have smiled at Basilia.

A spot of colour came into her cheeks then. She raised her chin and drew a deep breath. Her fists were clenched, but she held them down at her sides as if hoping I wouldn't notice. I watched her put on her courage like a cloak, and meet me with her head up.

'This is the princess Aoife of the Red Hair,' said Dermot Mac Murrough.

He was proud of her. His eyes told me.

There was soot on her face and her clothing was stained with mud and cinders, but Aoife was like a bright light in that dark place. She was tall and strongly built for a girl, and in her face was the pride of kings.

I was very pleasantly surprised. In marriage a man takes what he gets, because marriage is arranged to unite powerful families or to make new allies, and the daughters of important men are often plain. I hadn't expected anything more of this one.

But one thing was more important to me than her beauty.

Dermot had told me I would be his heir, I would succeed him as King of Leinster. Under English law, my marriage to his daughter made that certain. His crown would pass to me, I thought, and he had given me Aoife just as he would give me the crown. The two went together. Or so I thought.

I didn't know anything yet about Irish law.

Having seen and admired my bride-to-be, I began talking with Dermot Mac Murrough. The tall red-haired girl stood between us for a few moments, then added her voice to ours. Her Latin was just as good as mine, I was startled to discover.

'Why are you discussing my marriage as if I weren't here?' she wanted to know. 'I haven't yet said I would marry this man, Father.'

'Of course I'll marry her,' I told Dermot over her head.

Aoife stamped her foot. 'But I mightn't marry you!' she said directly to me.

I couldn't believe what I was hearing. How could a woman refuse to marry the man her father selected for her?

I looked at Dermot Mac Murrough. He wouldn't meet my eyes. 'What is this?' I asked.

My uncle coughed. 'Ah … there's something you should know, Richard. About these Irish.'

'What is it?' I asked impatiently. My men were staring at us.

'A woman must give permission to the marriage, you can't force her,' my uncle told me.

I was astonished. That was like asking a cow's permission before you bought it!

Raymond le Gros snorted with laughter. I turned to glare at him. Then I looked back at Aoife. She was watching me very closely. I felt as if she was weighing me in her mind.

I was in a strange country, among people with strange customs. It would be so easy to make a mistake and not even know I had done so.

If it was the custom among the Irish, it would surely do no harm to ask Aoife to marry me, I decided. It would be just a formality, of course. The marriage had long ago been agreed between her father and myself.

Or so I had thought. Watching her, I wasn't sure. She had a mind of her own, her eyes told me. She might well refuse me. This was a young woman who might well turn on her heel and walk away from me, leaving me alone with the men laughing at me.

I had never been in such a position before, not with a woman. I didn't want her to turn her back and walk away. Chewing the inside of my lip, I tried to think of the right words to say.

'Please,' I began. That sounded all right. 'Please.' It was easier the second time, but I mustn't beg. I was Strongbow, Norman knight, conqueror of Waterford. I swallowed hard. 'Marry me,' I said.

She was still looking at me with that measuring look. She unclenched her fists, and began playing with her long braids. For the first time I noticed something else, and I thought it was an Irish custom too. Long, narrow stones had been pushed through her plaits here and there. I wondered if the Irish thought that was beautiful. What an odd people!

I smiled at Aoife again, hopefully. I didn't know what else to do.

The silence had grown very long when at last she smiled back. Her face was indeed made for smiling. 'I shall marry you, Richard de Clare,' she decided.

Suddenly I felt as if I was standing in a beam of sunlight.

Until he let it out in a sigh, I didn't realise that Dermot had been holding his breath. She could have refused me, then, and he couldn't have forced her. The choice had been hers!

I had had a narrow escape.

There was talk then of the marriage to take place tomorrow. Aoife had her own ideas, and said what she thought. Irish women must be like that, I told myself.

'I want to be married in the cathedral, with the bishop,' Aoife said firmly.

'This cathedral?' Dermot asked.

'I would rather be married in Dublin, with Archbishop O'Toole giving us his blessing, Father, but Dublin is in the hands of your enemies,' Aoife replied. 'So Waterford will do.' She turned toward me. 'You're going to capture Dublin though, aren't you?'

'Of course I am. Er, we are,' I assured her.

She nodded, satisfied, and stopped toying with her hair.

That evening, while Waterford still smouldered, we held a council of war and agreed to march on Dublin next.

After my marriage to Aoife of the Red Hair.

Chapter 19
AOIFE

The Marriage of
Aoife and Strongbow

Long afterwards, people claimed I was radiantly beautiful on the day I married Richard de Clare. I don't remember what I looked like. I remember that the sun shone, and there were crowds of people. Even the defeated citizens of Waterford lined the lanes, hoping for a glimpse of the two of us. It would have been like a fair, had there not been the smell of smoke and death still hanging over the town.

There were no stones in my plaits on my wedding day. Indeed, my hair wasn't braided at all, but had been washed in water scented with French oil, and combed until it fell down my back in deep waves. My gown was of pale linen, set in a hundred pleats, and my shoes were of kidskin, soft and fine and sewn with gilded thread.

The bishop of Waterford, a stout man with a tonsure, married us. I don't remember the words he said. My mind kept playing tricks on me, thinking of other things. I recalled the day of Urla's wedding, and Conor and me eating stolen food and making ourselves sick. Thinking about it, I chuckled.

Richard heard me. He was standing beside me in his armour, polished for the occasion, and he was looking very serious.

'Why are you laughing?' he asked me in a whisper.

My Father, and the bishop, and so many noble warriors were all around us. I couldn't tell Richard about the stolen food, not then. So I merely said, 'Because I'm happy.' And to my surprise, it was true.

He gave me another smile then. 'And so am I,' he said wonderingly. 'I'll have a wife who laughs!'

We knelt before the bishop and Richard promised on his sword and his name and his honour to defend the Faith and to observe the obligations of marriage. I had no sword to swear on, but the bishop held the Psalter for me and I swore on God's words to be a good wife to my husband.

Then we prayed. Irish and Norman and Norseman together, Christians together, we knelt in God's house and prayed.

When we went out under the sky again, I was a married woman.

No sooner did I leave the cathedral than an attendant came running to me to bind up my hair. Married women shouldn't wear their hair loose.

But I hated having my hair bound. I pushed her away. 'I'm the wife of Strongbow now,' I said, 'and if I don't want my hair fastened, then I'll wear it down my back for as long as I like.'

The woman stared at me with wide eyes. But my new husband smiled. 'You have spirit,' he said.

I think he wasn't used to smiling. But every time he did, it came easier, so I tried to think of things that I could do to make him smile. When he wasn't scowling and looking serious he seemed almost young.

We held our wedding feast in what had been the hall of the executed Norse chieftain. This time I didn't have to steal the food. All the best morsels were put on my trencher of bread. While people all around us were eating and drinking, I told Richard about Urla's wedding and what had happened to Conor and me.

He threw back his head and burst into a great laugh that rang through the room. Hervey de Montmorency put down the chunk of roast meat he was eating and said in surprise, 'I never heard you laugh like that in your life, Richard!'

The man I had married replied, 'I never had such a woman beside me before, Uncle.'

I met Father's eyes across the table. He nodded his approval. 'Well done,' his lips told me silently.

And so my life changed. One day I was a child, the next, a married woman. In the polished metal mirror Father had given me as part of my dowry, I looked the same. I was the same person inside, too. But people looked at me differently.

I was Strongbow's wife.

When I went out into the streets of Waterford, people got out of my way. Wherever I went, a silence fell. Eyes followed me.

Already, the name of Strongbow was a weapon in Ireland. Stories of the fall of Waterford had been carried throughout the land, as fast as fire through dry grass.

There was one last meeting of the leaders of the invasion force, and Father, in Waterford. Women would not attend such a meeting, of course. But I did. When I told Richard that I meant to be present, he merely nodded.

'That's what Irish women do?' he asked.

'It's what I do,' I assured him.

I sat on the bench beside him, although not too close, for as usual when he appeared in public he was wearing his coat of mail. He had his iron helmet with him, too, but he never put that on unless he was going into battle. When I asked him why he said, 'It frightens people.'

So his helmet sat between us on the bench, like an eyeless iron skull. It didn't frighten me.

I listened with interest to the plans being made to attack Dublin.

'The High King claims the loyalty of Dublin and will try to protect it,' Father warned us, 'but I know a way through the mountains where no one keeps watch. We can march past Glendalough and be under the walls of Dublin before Rory O'Connor can do anything to stop us.'

After Richard and I retired for the night, he said, 'Your father is a clever man, Aoife. I hope I'll be as good a King of Leinster one day.'

'You? King of Leinster? What makes you think you could ever be King of Leinster?' I asked in astonishment.

It was his turn to be astonished. 'Don't you know? Under feudal law, by marrying you I become your father's heir.'

I was staring at him. 'Don't you know?' I echoed. 'Under Irish law – and you're in Ireland now – no man can acquire a kingdom through a woman, be it mother or wife.'

I thought his eyes would leap from his head. 'What are you saying? I don't believe you!'

'You can believe me,' I said smugly. 'Father gave me a fine education and I know the law.'

'He can't promise me his kingship?'

'Of course not. Irish kings are elected. The king who replaces him when he dies will be chosen from one of the royal line, either his most promising son or a kinsman of equal ability. Donal Mac Murrough Kavanaugh would probably be the first choice, because he's very popular with the Leinstermen. If not Donal, perhaps my uncle Murrough, who was named as King of Leinster in my father's place when –'

'Dermot lied to me!' cried Richard in a fury.

Now I saw his eyes flash with lightning. Now I saw the Strongbow who could freeze his enemies' blood with a glance!

Chapter 20
RICHARD

A Golden Land

The discovery that Dermot Mac Murrough had tricked me was a shock. He was a cheerfully cunning man, that I knew, but I hadn't expected he would deceive an ally he needed as he needed me.

'I suppose he had no choice,' Aoife told me. 'He would have offered you anything, I heard him say so.'

I didn't like to see my new wife taking her father's part. 'He promised me land he had lost, a daughter he didn't own, and a kingdom that wasn't his to give!' I was deeply shocked.

Aoife nodded. 'But you'll win that land back for him, the daughter has given herself to you, and every king must fight for and take his own kingdom, Richard. That's always the way. Surely your Henry has done the same?'

'How can one young head be so old in wisdom?'

'Father taught me that knowledge is power,' Aoife replied.

Ah, I thought. I should have learned that lesson myself, before I began this reckless adventure. I should have made a point of studying the Irish law. But I couldn't read. I would have had to rely on others to teach me, and where would I have found such a teacher?

And how would I have paid him?

Everything came back to my poverty. Aoife was right. I was in

Ireland now, and a king must fight for and take his own kingdom. If I wanted to end my poverty I would have to do it myself, in spite of the treachery of other men.

I couldn't even punish Dermot for his lie without hurting my wife, for I saw that she loved him. And I needed him to help me. He knew this land, I did not.

I didn't yet have a stronghold of my own to be the home of my new wife, and I didn't like to send her back to Dermot's stronghold. Nor did I dare leave her in Waterford.

'What am I going to do with you while we attack Dublin?' I wondered aloud.

Aoife grinned. 'I can go with you.'

'Women don't go to war,' I told her.

And then – as I was later to discover – she lied to me just as cheerfully as her father had done.

'They do in Ireland,' she said.

She was young and strong and determined, and there was really no reason to deny her. So I agreed, and named a company of guards to stay with her and protect her at all times. A leather tent was set aside for her use and we prepared to march on Dublin.

True to his word, for once, Dermot knew of an unguarded pass through the mountains south of that town. Word of our undertaking had already reached the High King, Rory O'Connor. O'Connor gathered an army of warriors from Brefni, Meath, and Connacht, and hurried toward Dublin. But we were there ahead of him.

Dermot sent word to the Archbishop of Dublin, Laurence O'Toole, who was his wife's brother, and urged him to persuade the Dubliners to surrender.

'When that happens, my uncle Laurence can give our marriage his blessing!' Aoife said happily.

She was still young enough to see things in the best possible light.

But I knew the capture of Dublin would be no simple matter. Still, if it could be done without too much bloodshed I would be thankful. The people of Waterford already hated us. I didn't want to give the people of Dublin reason to hate us also.

Speed was important. We must have Dublin's surrender before the High King's forces arrived in large enough numbers to overcome us.

Dermot Mac Murrough, as always, was cunning. 'I've asked the Archbishop to tell the Dubliners that while we have arrived, the High King has not. Let the townspeople think the High King is not coming to their rescue. They may well be willing to give up the town to us then.'

Some of my men were unhappy with this plan. 'If they just hand over the town to us, we can hardly loot it,' they complained to me.

'The whole purpose of this exercise is not to loot Dublin!' I exploded. My men were never easy to control, and now I felt them threatening to get away from me altogether. Seeing the wealth of Ireland, they had become greedy. Some of them enjoyed burning and smashing and destroying for its own sake. I worried about the damage they could do in this land, and the additional enemies they could make for me.

I spoke of this to Aoife. She was young, but she seemed to be interested in tactics, unlike any other woman I had ever known. She understood exactly what Dermot was trying to do and defended his idea. 'Listen to my father, Richard,' she said. 'He knows these people. Remember, you don't.'

I repeated her words to my men. 'We must trust Dermot's judgement in this,' I told them. I set my face in the mask of Strongbow to show them I wouldn't be moved, and at last they agreed.

We set up camp outside the walls. For men looking down upon us from the timbered walls of Dublin, we must have been an impressive sight. I had left a small company of warriors to hold Waterford, but the rest of my men were with us, including Raymond le Gros and his company. Dermot's followers were with us also. We had come through the mountains and past the sacred vale called Glendalough without losing a man, and our weapons were cleaned and shining in the autumn sun.

Soon enough, the gates of Dublin opened and the Archbishop came out to arrange a truce.

Aoife was delighted to see her uncle. She stood on the edge of the crowd of men while we talked about terms, and I saw Archbishop O'Toole nod to her when she caught his eye.

An agreement was made between Dermot and the Archbishop. Dublin was now Dermot's. There would be no looting, but in return for this the people of Dublin were to give Dermot Mac Murrough thirty hostages. If at any time in the future Dublin was no longer loyal to Dermot, those thirty hostages would die.

So the taking of Dublin had been a simple matter after all. Things were, I was learning, done differently in Ireland.

Dermot told me, 'We must make certain that the High King learns of this at once. When he knows Dublin is mine, and the terms, I don't think he will attack us. He won't want to lose a lot of valuable warriors for a lost cause.'

The message was sent to Rory O'Connor. As Dermot had expected, the High King and his armies turned around and went home.

In private, I said to my wife, 'Your father's cleverness wasn't the only reason why the High King withdrew, I think. Rory O'Connor is no stupid man, I'd say. He's not eager to face the warriors I brought with me. We have armour and weapons and ways of fighting he can't match, and he must know this.'

Aoife tossed her head. 'Our Irish warriors are as good as any of yours,' she said.

'Perhaps. But we have knights on horseback, and skilled archers, and our men fight in one unit, following one order. The Irish fight man by man, each according to his own desire. They cannot overcome one hundred men all following the same order.'

'Of course they can,' said Aoife.

But I could see that she was thinking about what I said. The next morning she was up with the larks, watching us drill our men in ways the Irish had never done.

I saw her nodding to herself. Aoife had a good mind. Perhaps the Irish were not as foolish as I thought, educating women!

The capture of Dublin was like drinking too much wine. Dermot Mac Murrough was drunk with success. He said to me, 'With your army at my back I could become High King of Ireland myself, and end the rule of the Connacht man!'

Yet even as we were celebrating our victory, things began to go wrong. I had told Aoife we fought to one order, but that was not strictly true. There are always men who disobey orders.

Two of my men – one of them my trusted Raymond le Gros! – would not accept the command to do no looting in Dublin. Secretly, they gathered two companies of followers and led them to opposite sides of the town without my knowledge. Then they broke down the walls and poured in upon the people, looting and slaughtering as they went.

I was furious! I ordered the leaders brought before me. But the damage was done. Now the Dubliners hated the Normans. They might remain loyal to Dermot as long as he held their hostages, but they couldn't be trusted not to put a knife in the back of any Norman they saw. Myself included.

'From now on, no Norman will walk through Dublin alone,' I ordered. 'Always go in pairs.'

To Raymond I said, 'I'll deal with you later.' At that moment I wanted to cut off his head, but he was my sister's husband. And I had promised Basilia I would take care of him.

I must content myself with stripping him of his loot.

In truth, this was a harsh penalty. Dublin was a very wealthy trading centre and Raymond had seized enough gold and furs and leathers to sink a small ship. He complained bitterly when I took it away from him. But we both knew he could soon get more. Ireland was rich beyond our wildest dreams.

Anyone of princely blood wore gold ornaments, and most of the Irish claimed princely blood. Even those who couldn't, wore silver and copper. The lowest servant had an iron ring or two, or the odd bit of amber on a thong, and good amber too, fine trading goods.

No one went hungry. The forests teemed with game. There was timber as far as the eye could see. Grassy meadowlands held more cattle than there were stars in the sky.

Ireland was a treasure house.

Compared to this island, Henry's England was as poor as I was myself. Many of its forests had long since been destroyed. The timber had gone to build houses and ships, or had been burned for charcoal. There was never enough food for the poor, and most people were poor. English weather was not as mild as Irish weather, and in a bad winter countless peasants died of cold and hunger.

Life in the land I had left was hard and short, brutal and cold.

But in Ireland, gold actually sparkled in the streams. I had seen it for myself, winking at me through the clear water.

As far as I was concerned, Ireland *was* gold. Ireland was the new fortune of the de Clares.

Chapter 21
AOIFE

Dermot Destroyed

How good it felt to be on the winning side! 'Chase O'Connor and take the high kingship away from him and give it to my father!' I urged Richard.

'No, Aoife,' he said. 'That would be reckless. We must make certain that the places we've already captured are firmly held.'

He said the same thing to Father, who didn't like it any more than I did. Father could almost taste the high kingship.

Richard told him, 'I intend to go back to Waterford for the winter and build earthworks and strongholds there. Then in the spring I'll be in a strong position for more fighting.'

'No!' Father argued. 'If we don't pursue the High King now we'll have lost a priceless opportunity!'

'You want revenge,' Richard said. 'I want something more solid than that. I've risked everything to come here, I don't want to lose it all now just to give you the pleasure of holding a knife to Rory O'Connor's throat.'

'Make him see my side, Aoife,' Father pleaded with me.

I was torn between them. I understood how Father felt because I felt the same way myself. But this time … this time, I suspected Richard was right.

And he was my husband. At last I took his side. I had given my word to God at our marriage.

When I told Father I wouldn't argue his case with my husband he looked very sad. 'Only bad things can come of a daughter's failing to stand up for her father,' he said. 'But very well; I'll do what must be done, myself.' He put one hand to either side of my face and pulled me to his lips for a kiss. 'God's blessing on you, Aoife,' he said. Then he left me with Richard.

We returned to Waterford, where Richard began the building of forts and strongholds. Messengers brought us news of Father almost every week, however, and Richard always shared it with me.

We learned that the High King had reminded my father of the treaty by which he had been allowed the freedom of Leinster, and demanded that he send away his hired warriors and give up warring.

Father proudly – and recklessly – replied that he would do no such thing. He went even further. He swore to keep fighting until he had claimed the monarchy of all Ireland.

Aflame with success, Father and his loyal Leinstermen set out across Meath. His true target, I knew, was his old enemy, O'Rourke of Brefni. Father thundered across the countryside, battering Clonard and burning Kells on his way. On reaching Brefni he took prisoners and cattle, but didn't succeed in capturing Tiernan O'Rourke, who escaped.

O'Rourke fled to Rory O'Connor.

'This is frightening news,' I told Richard. 'When Father made that treaty with the High King he was forced to give hostages of good conduct. My own brother, Conor, and Donal Mac Murrough Kavanaugh's son were among them.

'Father was so certain they'd be safe. The High King has never personally done harm to any of our family.'

'Your brother Enna was blinded,' Richard reminded me. He had begun learning all he could of events in Ireland. He seemed determined to become as Irish as any of us.

'Enna was held by another tribe, not by the High King,' I explained. 'They were our enemies too, and allies of the High King. But Rory O'Connor had no control over what they did.'

'Yet now you're frightened for the hostages the High King holds?'

'I am indeed,' I said, 'because Tiernan O'Rourke is with the High King. He hates Father so much, and he has the High King's ear. He could persuade him to do … anything.'

He did. My worst fears came true.

According to Irish law, hostages must be kept in as much comfort as their hosts. Conor and Donal's son and another lad, foster-kin of ours, had been well fed and well housed while living in the High King's household in Connaught. Conor had even planned a marriage with the High King's daughter.

Then my father trailed his coat in front of the High King and Tiernan O'Rourke, and old anger burst into new flame. O'Rourke must have argued long and hard to get him to do it, but at last the High King gave the order.

The three hostages were slain beside the Shannon river at Athlone, and their heads were sent to my father.

Even Strongbow was shocked. 'What sort of people are you?' he demanded of me.

'Why don't you ask what sort of person Tiernan O'Rourke is? He's to blame for this, I know it! He spent years and years trying to get even with my father, and now he's done it. He's a monster, oh, he's a monster!' I cried, sobbing.

Broken by the news, Father was returning to Ferns. I had to be with him. I didn't ask Richard for permission. I simply told him I was going. I would meet Father and join him in his grief.

My husband ordered a company of his warriors to go with me, and we set off through winter-bleak countryside for the palace that had once been my home.

When I saw Father I hardly knew him. Donal was trying to be brave about his loss, but Father was destroyed. His hair had gone almost white, and he had the face of a man of ninety. He shuffled when he walked, and moved his lips even when he wasn't talking. It broke my heart to see him.

I couldn't find it in me to blame him for the recklessness and ambition that had brought this disaster upon us. He was suffering enough already.

Mor was still blaming everything on Dervorgilla. She spoke of nothing else. My mother, who now had a dead son and a blind one, wouldn't speak at all. She went to her bed and never said another word to my father as long as she lived.

Only a few weeks before, Father had been swelled with victory and full of life. Now anyone could see he was dying. His years had caught up with him all at once.

I walked with him through the grounds of Ferns and tried to talk of pleasant things, but he paid no attention to me.

'How grand everything looks now, Father,' I said as cheerfully as I knew how. 'You've made Ferns more beautiful than ever.'

He didn't look at me. He mumbled something, but I couldn't make out any words.

'Will you build some more?' I asked, trying to get him to talk.

He shrugged. He stared off into space.

What could I say to him? How could I comfort him? I couldn't even comfort myself. Tears began leaking down my cheeks.

Father stopped, turned to me, looked at me dimly, and said, 'My merry Aoife. Why don't you laugh any more?'

Then he laughed, an awful cracked sound that chilled me to my soul. He laughed and the laughter broke into a thousand pieces and became great deep sobs I couldn't bear to hear.

I fled back to Richard. I couldn't stand the sight of Ferns.

I spent the bleak months of winter helping my husband fortify his new holdings. He stayed in contact with my uncle, the Archbishop of Dublin, and there was talk between them of building a new cathedral.

'God will bless us in Ireland if we do this,' Richard told me.

But I recalled the churches and monasteries Father had built, and wasn't so sure. 'God cannot be bought,' I told Richard.

Then a message came to us from England. Word had reached King Henry of my husband's successes in Ireland. In fact, he had been told that Strongbow was now master of Leinster and other territories.

To the English king, it must have sounded as if my husband was grabbing everything he could. Henry's response was swift. He immediately sent out a notice that no more ships should leave England for Ireland, and that all his subjects now in Ireland should return to England before Easter, on pain of losing all they possessed and being banished forever.

A messenger read this notice aloud to my husband, in the English tongue. I saw Richard's eyes go cold. He told me what the king was demanding.

'Will you go back?' I asked. 'You have a castle there. And kin.'

My husband didn't answer. Instead he walked to the arrowslit of the new stronghold we were building in a place called Kilkenny, and gazed out across the land. 'I have a son and daughter there,' he said. 'But I've already sent back enough riches from Ireland to provide for them.'

'Don't you worry about them?' I wanted to know. 'My father always worried about his children. Don't you at least long to see yours again?'

'We were never very close,' he said sadly. 'I dare say they're not eager to see me.'

It was the first time he had spoken to me of his other family. I hadn't asked about them. I didn't want to think about them. I wanted Richard to be just mine.

But now the ice was broken. 'What was your first wife like?' I asked.

He smiled with one side of his mouth only. 'Nothing like you, Aoife. I didn't know what it meant to be happy until I came to Ireland.' He put one hand on my shoulder, so very gently. If only the people who called him Strongbow could have seen him in that moment!

'All the riches I want are here,' he said.

Richard had a scribe write his reply to the English king: 'My Lord, it was with your licence, as I understood, that I came to Ireland for the purpose of helping Dermot Mac Murrough recover his kingdom. Whatever lands I have had the good fortune to acquire in this country, either from Dermot or any other person, I owe to your gracious favour and I shall hold them at your disposal.'

Richard had the letter read to him several times, until he was happy with the wording. Then he ordered Raymond le Gros to carry it personally to King Henry.

'What will happen now?' I asked my husband.

'I don't know,' he said.

Chapter 22
RICHARD

A New King in Leinster

The Archbishop of Dublin sent word to me that a Synod of the clergy had been held at Armagh. The topic was the invasion by myself and the other Anglo-Normans. The clergy decided that we were the divine vengeance sent by God to punish the Irish for their sins.

I had never thought of myself as an instrument of God. Nor had I any desire to punish the Irish. The longer I lived among them, the more I liked them. Their songs and their food and their customs all appealed to me. I felt more at home in Ireland among the Irish than I had ever done in Pembrokeshire, though I couldn't say why.

Perhaps it was because of Aoife.

Aoife was very worried about her father, and for her sake I worried also. I had a foothold in Ireland now, I could survive without Dermot Mac Murrough, but when we heard that he was dying I was almost as upset as my wife.

We galloped to Ferns on our fastest horses. We found his entire family – all who survived – gathered there, including his son-in-law, Donal O'Brien, who was King of Thomond now.

As we crossed the courtyard I could hear people whispering already. 'Who will be King of Leinster when Dermot is dead?' they were asking each other behind their hands.

The question seemed to hang in the air. I felt a knot gather in my belly.

I had tried to learn as much as I could about Irish law. As Aoife had told me, Dermot could not make me a king, and neither could my marriage to his daughter. Yet if Norman feudal law prevailed in Ireland, I would be the new King of Leinster.

I should be. That was what Dermot had wanted, had promised me. He had controlled southeastern Ireland for forty-six years.

It was my turn now.

When we gathered around the dying man's bed, I looked at the other faces. His brother Murrough. His son Donal Mac Murrough Kavanaugh. Murtough, Murrough's son. Three strong men, each wanting to be king. One would be elected. Elected!

It was a mad way to choose a leader, I thought. Of all the Irish customs, this was one that must go.

The man who lay on the bed, his breath barely lifting his chest, was only sixty-one years old but he looked much older. As I bent over him he opened his eyes.

'Strongbow? Is that you?'

I leaned closer so his dimming sight would know me. The other three men frowned. I knew then that they didn't want me any closer to Dermot.

'I'm here,' I told the dying king. I leaned even closer, so no one else could hear when I said, 'I've come to remind you of your promise.'

Weak though he was, he understood. Dermot's brain never stopped working. 'The kingship,' he said hoarsely.

'The kingship,' I agreed. 'The time has come for the transfer of power. Tell these men who stand by your bed that I'm to be the next King of Leinster.'

Dermot tried to draw a deep breath, and coughed. Donal Mac

Murrough Kavanaugh reached out and caught my arm.

'Leave him alone,' he said warningly.

I lost my temper. 'I brought this man victory!' I roared. 'I have a right to be here, and to ask a reward of him!'

Dermot found enough breath to speak then. 'Victory,' he said in a hollow voice, as if he didn't know what the word meant. 'Victory? You're wrong, Strongbow. My life has been ... a disaster from beginning to end.'

He closed his eyes, and died on the next breath.

I presume his soul went to God. How his Maker judged him, I can't say. But he was gone, and I was no nearer to being King of Leinster than I was the day I first set foot in Ireland.

Aoife's grief was terrible to see. The other women were all crying, but she didn't cry. Her pain was in her eyes and wouldn't spill out, but stayed there. Every time I looked at her I could see it.

'I cried for Enna and Conor,' she told me. 'Father deserves something more.'

The night Dermot died, she tore out great handfuls of her heavy red hair. I found them strewn about our chamber, like rushes on the floor.

The next day Donal Mac Murrough Kavanaugh came to me. 'If my father wanted you to be King of Leinster,' he said, 'I won't vote against you.' I never forgot that gesture. I realised then that he loved his father as much as Aoife did. Dermot was a man to envy, having children who loved him so.

He was laid to rest in the churchyard of the cathedral at Ferns that he had supported in his lifetime. Once he was dead, many harsh things were said about him, some of them by the clergy. But I never heard his children say a word against him.

I took my wife back to the south and tried to comfort her. But soon I needed comforting.

Dermot had died on the first of May. The king to replace him was elected within a month. It was Dermot's nephew, Murtough, who was of the noble line and a devout Christian man. The clergy wanted someone with a blameless reputation to succeed Dermot Mac Murrough, and their influence on the voting chieftains was very strong.

The news hit me like a thunderbolt. 'This isn't what Dermot wanted! He promised me! *He promised me!*' I raved to Aoife.

'He promised what he had no right to promise,' she reminded me. 'You must be reasonable, Richard.'

I couldn't be reasonable. 'I don't care,' I said like an angry child. 'He promised me!'

What could I do? How was I going to get back what had been taken from me?

Then Raymond le Gros returned to Ireland with still more bad news. 'King Henry wishes you to know that he insists on your return to England. It's a command.'

'Is it now?' I folded my arms across my chest. 'What Henry wants isn't that important any more. The kingship of Leinster means more to me than a command from Henry Plantagenet.'

'You defy the king at your peril,' Raymond warned me.

'This whole venture has been at my peril!' I reminded him. 'And the only way I'll claim my reward for my danger is to stay here and fight. For Ireland, not for England. England's little more than a memory to me now.'

'It's your home,' Raymond said.

'Not any more. If it ever was. I've built strongholds for myself around the borders of the land that I claim here, and those are my homes now. When I travel to Kilkenny, or Kildare, or Dublin, the natives treat me with respect.

'No one in England ever treated me with that much respect, Raymond. Murtough might be King of Leinster, but the name of

Strongbow is on every tongue. All Ireland is watching and waiting to see what I'll do next.

'Whatever it is, I won't be going back to England,' I assured him.

In truth, I didn't know what to do. Dermot's death had left me in a most awkward position. While he lived, I could be considered his chosen heir. Now that he was dead and another man ruled Leinster, I was no more than a leader of foreign mercenaries.

Aoife knew how miserable I was. 'You should make your peace with my cousin Murtough,' she suggested. 'Our family has always stood together. Even when we quarrel among ourselves, we don't break apart. You're of my family now. Go to Murtough and offer to be his strong right arm as you were my father's. Even if you aren't King of Leinster, you can be a power in Leinster.'

'You speak wisely,' I admitted, 'but it's hard for me to bend the knee to the man who's king in my place.'

'Had you rather go back to England and bend your knee to Henry?' Aoife asked shrewdly.

So I left her in safekeeping on the Slaney with Robert FitzStephen and rode for Ferns, as she wanted.

Murtough welcomed me most kindly. He knew what I was feeling. But he was indeed a good Christian man, he didn't gloat. We had a long talk together and parted as friends, though several times I had to bite my tongue to keep from saying bitter words I would regret later.

When I left Ferns, I felt better. Murtough was not as strong a man as Dermot had been. When the time came, he could be shouldered aside gracefully.

From Ferns we rode to Dublin to learn how work was progressing on the new cathedral. Seeing Christ Church rise, Irish timber upon a foundation of Irish stone, I began to feel more hopeful. I was building for the future in a number of ways.

I knelt in the unfinished cathedral amid the smells of raw timber and stone dust, and bowed my head. I didn't speak to God, but to my father. What I said was not a prayer, but one last plea for my father's approval.

'I defended our property and name as best I could in England,' I told him. 'But now I've won new land and new honour in Ireland. Be proud of me.'

The church was very silent. My words to my father in heaven echoed in my head.

As I left the cathedral, a sentry shouted from the wall that surrounded Dublin, 'The High King is said to have left Connacht! He's marching this way with a mighty army!'

Chapter 23

AOIFE

Waiting for News

'Come with me to Murtough and help make peace between us,' Richard had urged me. But I wouldn't. It was the first thing I'd ever refused him. But I couldn't bear to go back to Ferns so soon, there were too many sad memories there. So I insisted on staying behind.

Robert FitzStephen was happy to have Strongbow's wife as his guest, and promised to lift my spirits with feasting and entertainments until Richard returned to me. But when the days dragged by with no word from my husband, I began to worry.

FitzStephen laughed at me. 'What sort of man reports to his wife? Come, Aoife, put on that smile of yours and I'll take you out hunting with my new falcon.'

I went to please him, but in truth I didn't like the Norman sport of falconry very much. It seemed unnatural. We Irish hunted the red deer with hounds, which the hounds enjoyed as much as the hunters did. But falconry was different. The poor falcons were bound with thongs and kept blinded most of the time with hoods over their heads. They didn't even get to eat any of the meat they caught. Like the poorest captives, they were given only a hunk of rotten horsemeat.

And there were so many laws and rules about falconry! All those petty details didn't make any difference, as far as I could see. Yet the

Normans got very upset if even the tiniest rule was ignored.

It was a ridiculous amount of trouble to catch one sparrow that any good Irish slinger could have brought down with a stone. But when I said as much to FitzStephen, he scowled at me.

'You people simply don't understand,' he said.

After that I stopped trying to please him. I spent my days waiting for Richard. At last a passing Leinsterman told us he and his captains had gone on to Dublin. Then for a while longer we heard nothing else, until we learned that the High King was marching toward Dublin with an army.

The marrow froze in my bones. 'He means to kill my husband!' I told FitzStephen. 'You must go to Dublin at once with all your men!'

The Norman knight agreed with me. But before he could gather his warriors, we were attacked ourselves!

The Norsemen came out of the night. They surrounded the earthwork fort FitzStephen was holding and kept us penned inside like animals.

Chapter 24

RICHARD

Siege at Dublin

When I first arrived in Dublin, the Archbishop greeted me and took me aside to speak to me privately. He talked about the Synod of Armagh, and said very harsh things about the actions of my men in Ireland. 'You're looting our land,' he said, 'and it must stop. You should return to your own land.'

'This is mine,' I told him. 'Dermot meant me to be King of Leinster.'

Laurence O'Toole grew angry. 'Even building a cathedral does not give you a right to Irish kingship!'

That night, without my knowing, he sent word to the High King, asking Rory O'Connor to bring an army to Dublin and drive out the Anglo-Normans.

During the following days, while I was inspecting parts of Dublin and the area outside the walls, the Archbishop avoided me. When I visited the new cathedral he was nowhere in sight. I should have wondered about this, but my mind was busy with many things.

Then we learned that the High King was marching toward us with an army. The clever old fox had also sent word to some of his Norse allies, who were approaching Dublin from the sea. We were to be caught between them and destroyed!

I sent a hasty message to Robert FitzStephen, ordering him to gather his men in the south and come to our aid at once.

But I got no reply.

I had to work swiftly. Gathering my own men together, I gave strict orders. No one was to act on his own. Each person was to follow the chain of command in the Norman style, acting according to one plan.

Our enemies didn't work to one plan, however. That was not their way. The Norse arrived long before the High King, and swept into Dublin Bay in their longships, carrying battle axes and thirsty for blood. Our sentries on the wall of the town counted as many as sixty ships, and thought there might be a thousand men.

We were ready for them. When they stormed the eastern gate, we met them with two companies of horse. We caught them between one company and the other and broke their attack. My knights on horseback simply ran over them.

The Norsemen fled back to their ships, defeated. But we had no time to celebrate. The High King's forces arrived almost at once, in much greater numbers, and encamped along the Liffey.

I called my captains together.

'I think the High King will do what I'd do in his position,' I told them. 'He'll lay siege to the town. He'll try to deny us food and water and starve us out. Go to the storehouses of Dublin and see what supplies we have.'

They came back to me with long faces.

'There's enough food for the townspeople until the harvest is in, but no more.'

It was then July. And with the High King's army waiting outside the walls, the harvest of the countryside couldn't be brought to us when it was gathered at the end of summer.

I ordered no man to eat more than he must to keep body and soul together, and we waited. Beyond the walls, Rory O'Connor and his allies waited. From time to time my men stood atop the walls and we hurled spears and curses at each other.

The High King allowed no messenger into Dublin. I had no word of FitzStephen, or of my wife. I had no word of anything beyond the walls. It was like being in a dungeon. Every day I paced through the town, unable to be still, and the Dubliners stood in their doorways and stared at me. Their dogs ran out to yap at me and tried to bite my legs.

When I came across the Archbishop I gave him a glare of cold fury and said nothing to him. He retreated inside his cathedral – that I had built for him – and said nothing to me.

It couldn't go on forever. At last a messenger came from the High King, offering to talk through Archbishop O'Toole.

An offer to talk was better than starving in silence, so I sent for Aoife's uncle. 'Go to Rory O'Connor,' I told him, 'and offer him these, my terms for surrender. Tell him I shall recognise him as my king, and in return shall hold my own kingdom of Leinster for him.'

O'Toole was shocked. 'You are not King of Leinster! You cannot hold it for anyone!'

My friend, Maurice FitzGerald was shocked. 'You're already holding Leinster for the King of England!' he reminded me.

'Just do as I say,' I told the Archbishop, 'or see the people of Dublin starve to death and know it's your fault.'

He set out to talk to the High King. We waited, not knowing what to expect.

In time the Archbishop returned. 'I am instructed to tell you that unless you surrender everything you hold and agree to depart from Ireland on a given day with all your forces, the High King will attack without delay and destroy Dublin, and you in it. All will be burned to the ground, yourselves included.'

I had to plan. But men were pressing around me, urging this action and that, making it hard to think.

Then someone else slipped into the town through the small gate that had been opened for the Archbishop.

It was Donal Mac Murrough Kavanaugh!

I was desperately glad to see him, though less so when I heard his news. 'Robert FitzStephen is also under siege in the fort of Carrick, and can't come to you,' he said. 'My sister Aoife is with him.'

'Is she safe?'

'I don't know. She was, when last I heard, but that's been several days.'

What to do? Now that the Norsemen had left the harbour, I could perhaps have got a ship out and sent word to King Henry, pleading for help. But I doubted that he would help me. To him I was a traitor. I had refused his command to give up the adventure in Ireland.

Unable to decide what to do, I consulted my most trusted knights. 'Shall we try to get word to Henry?' I asked them.

Maurice FitzGerald replied, 'Can we expect any aid from our own country? I tell you we can't. The truth is, to the English we're Irish now, and to the Irish we're English. Whatever is done we must do for ourselves.'

There spoke a man who had no home to return to, a man who, like myself, meant Ireland for his home now.

FitzGerald's bold words put the heart back into me.

'Very well. We'll fight,' I said. 'And if we're to have any chance of winning, we must be the first to attack. They won't expect that of us, after this long siege.'

We slipped out of Dublin by the east gate shortly before midday. Raymond le Gros led the way with twenty mounted knights, followed by a company of foot soldiers, then thirty more knights on horseback. The rest of our foot soldiers came next, then I brought up the rear with forty more knights.

We swept around to the southwest, then at my order split into two groups, attacking the High King's armies at encampments at Castleknock and Kilmainham.

We fell upon them like hornets.

Far from expecting us, they were relaxing in warm autumn sunshine. Some, including the High King himself, were bathing in the Liffey. He had a very narrow escape and fled with his dignity in tatters.

I fought as I had never fought before. I was fighting for everything that mattered to me, my new land, my new wife, my new life. It would be better to die than to lose them.

When a man is not afraid to die he becomes a terrible warrior indeed.

We savaged the High King's army. We killed them in the river, we killed them on the shore. We killed them as they sat on the ground beside their cooking fires, with food in their mouths.

The High King's army broke and ran.

We took their abandoned supplies, we took the weapons they left scattered on the grass.

We took everything we wanted.

Chapter 25
AOIFE

Holding Out

My half-brother, Donal Mac Murrough Kavanaugh, tried to visit me and discovered our danger. Somehow he got through the enemy lines, and was welcomed into the fort.

'You're being besieged by Norsemen from Wexford,' he told us. 'They're loyal to the High King these days. They hate the Normans and reject their claims to Wexford.'

'I don't have enough men to fight them off,' FitzStephen said. 'Can you get back through their lines and send word to Strongbow?'

Donal shook his head. 'That's why I'm here. I came to tell you that Strongbow is also under siege by the High King, in the town of Dublin. That's probably why you're trapped here, to keep you from going to his aid.'

How I hated the High King in that moment!

'If you got in to us, you can get out,' I told Donal. 'You must go to Dublin. Find a way to join my husband and help him fight. He'll win, I know he will. Then he can rescue us.'

Donal was uncertain.'I don't like to leave you in such a desperate situation.'

'We'll be all right for a while,' FitzStephen assured him. 'These walls are thick and my archers are deadly. Just hurry, will you? In the name of God, hurry!'

The next time I saw Donal Mac Murrough Kavanaugh he came riding boldly up to the gates of the fort beside my husband and Maurice FitzGerald, all of them under triumphant Norman banners.

'We've defeated the High King of Ireland, Aoife!' Richard cried as soon as he saw me. Our besiegers had scattered in every direction at his approach, and now the fort stood open in welcome to the victors.

How we celebrated that night!

Chapter 26
RICHARD

A Rival to Henry II

With one bold stroke, I had won an unexpected victory against the High King of Ireland himself. He and his allies were thrown into confusion. Only Dermot's old enemy Tiernan O'Rourke still had some fight left in him. He mounted another attack on Dublin, but was soundly defeated by my men and his oldest son was killed.

We swept through Leinster, putting down pockets of resistance. Robert FitzStephen was taken prisoner and treated cruelly by some Wexford men. Each day brought a new battle. But we were winning. We could feel it, like a drumbeat growing louder and louder.

Then my uncle came to me, very worried. 'Your latest success has made the King of England more angry than ever,' he said. 'Henry thinks you and your knights are seizing Ireland for yourselves, and that you mean to set up here as a rival king.'

A thrill went through me at those words. Richard de Clare, a rival king to Henry Plantagenet! But I was too old and had seen too much to really believe it. I knew Henry's strength. More importantly, I knew how swiftly he would break such a rival.

'I must go to him myself,' I decided. 'I must once more submit to his royal will, and convince him I hold Ireland only in his name.'

'It may be too late,' my uncle warned me. 'He's gathering an army of invasion even as we speak.'

I could lose everything.

I made hasty preparations and set out for England, leaving my best captains and most loyal knights to hold the lands we had won in Ireland, and to protect my wife.

Aoife was indignant. 'I can protect myself, Richard!'

I had to laugh. She could always make me laugh. 'Then let's say I'm leaving some men with you to protect my enemies from you!'

She laughed too. It was very hard to leave her.

Sailing across the Irish Sea a second time was just as bad as the first. I arrived with a belly that ached from heaving, and the taste of vomit still in my mouth.

The king was holding court on the Welsh border, I learned on my arrival. He had moved swiftly indeed. He was determined that Ireland should not be a new kingdom in our control. He had already put together a fleet of two hundred and fifty vessels at Milford Haven, and gathered an army to transport across the sea to Ireland. The flower of his knighthood was with them.

At first Henry refused to see me. But I told everyone within hearing, even the littlest pages of his court, how loyal I was to him and how eager I was to lay my conquests at his feet. At last he sent for me.

My position had changed since the last time I entered the royal presence. Then I came almost as a beggar. Now I came as a conqueror.

Henry had changed too. He was grey, not in the hair but in the face, and his eyes were haunted. I had learned that he was almost at war with Rome, over the murder of the Archbishop, Thomas à Becket. So much had happened while I was in Ireland, and none of it had seemed important to me, over there.

I bent my knee to him and bowed my head. He stared down at me for a long time without saying anything. I could feel my heart beating heavily. I wondered if he could hear it.

I wondered if he would draw his sword and strike my head from my shoulders. He was a king. To him, I was a traitor.

At last I heard him draw a deep breath. 'You have done well in Ireland, I believe?'

'I have, Your Majesty. In your name,' I added quickly. 'I have subdued many of the natives.'

'But not all of them.'

'Not all of them,' I had to admit. 'I had too few men to conquer the entire island.'

I dared to look up at him then. Henry was smiling.

'I have enough men,' he said.

My heart sank in me.

We talked long into the night. Henry was more kindly disposed towards me than I had expected. He always did admire a victor. In the end, we reached an agreement that sat heavy on me, but it was the best I could do. I would hand over to the English king Dublin, Waterford, Wexford, and those other lands he might name, but he would allow me to continue to hold for myself the strongholds I had built and the lands around them.

Compared to the kingship of Leinster it was not a great prize, but at least it was in Ireland.

As I had always known, the King of England meant Ireland itself to be his. The Normans who had followed me and fought with me would be granted lands and titles in this new kingdom, provided they paid tribute to England and held Henry, not Rory O'Connor, as their king.

I returned home, to Ireland, to await Henry's arrival. I didn't have long to wait.

We did, however, receive one bit of news during that time that brought great cheer into my camp and to my wife. We learned that Tiernan O'Rourke had engaged one of my knights, Hugh de Lacy, in battle in Meath. O'Rourke had been killed, and his head hung over the gates of Dublin.

When we heard this, Aoife went around smiling for the rest of the day.

De Lacy set about building himself a castle at Trim in the Norman fashion, to celebrate.

I daresay Dermot Mac Murrough lay warm and happy in his tomb. My wife kept the tomb wreathed with flowers, for as long as the summer lasted.

The autumn brought Henry Plantagenet.

Chapter 27

AOIFE

The Visit of Henry

'I want to go with you to meet the king,' I told Richard firmly.

'It's not done,' he said. 'You're a woman.'

'I'm a princess of Leinster and the daughter of a king!' I shot back. 'And furthermore, I'm your wife.'

'Ah, but what am I?' Richard asked sadly.

I gave him the title I knew he treasured most. 'You're Strongbow,' I said.

I went with him to meet the king.

The King of the English landed near Waterford in October in the Year of Our Lord 1171. He brought five hundred horsemen and thirty-five hundred men-at-arms.

With the exception of Rory O'Connor and his most loyal allies, the princes of Ireland went to greet him. The hosting of such an important king – with so many warriors – was an event of major importance. The Irish princes were awed by the size of the force he had brought. Here truly was a king to put Rory O'Connor into the shade! The High King's star had all but set anyway, since my husband's defeat of him.

'I'll present you to him. Remember, you're just a woman.'

I glared at my husband. There was still too much of the Norman left in him to please me.

I had no chance to speak to Henry anyway, as it happened. From the moment he set foot on Irish soil he was surrounded by a great party of warriors and courtiers. A glittering canopy of cloth-of-gold was set up over his head wherever he halted. Henry strode the earth as if he was better than any of us, gazing neither to the left nor the right. A great train of followers bustled after him wherever he went.

My sister Urla arrived with her husband, Donal Mor O'Brien. 'We have come to give our formal submission to this new High King and promise the usual tribute,' Urla told me. She and her husband didn't see any difference between Henry of England and Rory O'Connor of Connaught.

In fact, Donal O'Brien was pleased with Henry's arrival. 'A man that strong is useful,' he told Richard. 'I can hire some of his Normans to fight for me.'

Henry began a royal progress towards Dublin. He went slowly, allowing the natives plenty of time to see how many warriors he had. As the great High King Brian Boru had once done, Henry frightened people into submission through sheer weight of numbers. He didn't have to fight any battles.

On the day he set out on his royal progress, Henry summoned my husband. Richard went alone to meet him. I waited fearfully. I knew Richard was worried. I wished he had taken me with him. It's much easier to know the worst right away, than to have to wait for it.

When Richard returned late that night his face was deeply lined with weariness. But he managed a small smile for me. 'I'm still alive, at least,' he said bravely.

'And?'

'And that's about all, Aoife. In return for my total submission to him, Henry is giving me only our stronghold in Kilkenny and a few other bits and pieces. Nothing compared to what I fought so hard to win.'

Richard's eyes were filled with pain. I put my hand on his arm. 'Henry is making a mistake,' I said angrily. 'He's a fool, there's no better man than you in Ireland, and he should reward you lavishly for what you've done. If I had been with you, I would have told him!' I stamped my foot and tossed my head.

In spite of himself, my husband smiled. 'That's exactly why you weren't with me. I can't imagine Henry letting some Irish woman call him a fool to his face. He'd have clapped me in irons at once.' His smile widened into a grin that drove some of the pain from his eyes. 'And maybe it would have been worth it,' he added, 'just to see my brave wife attack the King of England.'

But he didn't really mean it. I knew that.

'What about the kingship of Leinster, Richard?'

My husband sighed. 'Although he won't actually adopt the title, the new King of Leinster is Henry Plantagenet now. And because of O'Brien's submission to him, he's overlord of Munster as well. My men and I won the battles, but he's won Ireland.'

The English king insisted that his Anglo-Norman subjects in Ireland must obey English law, not Irish, and must remain loyal to England. To those he considered loyal enough he gave grants of land. Hugh de Lacy was given Meath and the command of Dublin.

'Giving him Dublin is meant as a punishment for me,' my husband raged. But there was nothing he could do about it.

King Henry also gave the town of Dublin a charter. Under this charter, he granted Dublin to the citizens of Bristol rather than to the Norse.

I thought Richard would rebel. I hoped Richard would rebel, as my father would have done.

But Richard was tired. He was not a young man when he arrived in Ireland, and he had endured a most difficult year. Like the rest of our men, he was awed by Henry's army.

As a warning, perhaps, to Richard, Henry punished Robert FitzStephen. FitzStephen had been handed over to the invading English king by the Wexford men in an effort to win Henry's favour. Henry spared Robert's life, but stripped him of all that Richard had given him and sent him into a bitter exile in the far west of Ireland, to try to hack a place for himself in the wilderness.

To hold them in his name, Henry put garrisons of loyal men into Dublin, Wexford, and Waterford. He spent the winter in Dublin in a new timber palace built for him, and the Norman knights attended him there, my husband among them.

Chapter 28
RICHARD

Tales of Aoife's Deeds

On the surface, Henry was kind enough to me. He treated me as he did his other nobles. He had a place held for me at his banquet table. He even allowed me to parcel out bits of land to some of my most deserving followers.

But I had no real power. He knew it and I knew it.

I went alone to the new cathedral, and bowed my head once more in the echoing silence.

'I'm not to be King of Leinster after all,' I whispered in defeat to my father. 'But I did my best. You know I did my best.'

As usual, it wasn't enough.

At the start of Lent, in the Year of Our Lord 1172, Henry left Dublin for Wexford. He stayed there until Easter. Then he set sail for England, never to return.

But the Ireland he left behind him was changed forever.

England was now in control of most of the east and of much of the midlands as well. New castles were springing up everywhere, great grim stone piles in the Norman fashion, reminding me of the home that had been mine in Pembrokeshire.

I spent my time trying to strengthen my grip on what little had been left to me. Aoife was the rock beneath my feet. Loyal, strong, never complaining, she helped me in all I did.

I urged my fellow knights to take Irish women for their wives. 'You can do no better anywhere,' I assured them.

Raymond le Gros, fortunately, preferred my sister Basilia. He made another trip across the Irish Sea and brought her home to Ireland. How glad I was then that I had given her to Raymond, in spite of his faults. If she had not been married to him I would never have seen her again.

'Let me hug you!' I cried when I first saw her. I took her into my arms and squeezed as hard as I could, the way Aoife liked.

'You're crushing me, Richard,' Basilia protested against my chest.

She was shy with me. We had been apart for a long time and both our lives had changed.

'What do you think of my sister?' I asked Aoife proudly.

'She's very pretty. But can't she speak any language except the Norman tongue? I've learned a lot of Norman, but not enough to chatter away with her as I would like. And she doesn't even know any Latin!'

'We don't teach our women languages,' I said.

Aoife gave me a look of disgust.

I had always thought of Basilia as a beauty. Next to my Aoife, however, she seemed like a pale lily beside a glowing rose. Basilia was shy, Aoife was outspoken. Basilia was frail, Aoife was strong. Basilia could make me smile, but Aoife could make me laugh no matter how bad I felt.

So I had my sister back with me – in a way. My son and daughter remained in England. The loot I had sent them from Ireland provided well for them. My daughter would have a titled husband someday; I could do no more for her.

I kept my head down, worked hard, and tried not to be bitter.

When the most recent messenger arrived from the king, at first I couldn't believe him. 'You are asked to use your sword in His Majesty's service,' I was informed.

'Henry summons me to fight in his name!' I exclaimed to Aoife. 'It's a good sign!'

'Is it?' Aoife raised one eyebrow doubtfully. She was her father's daughter, suspicious and wary. 'I think he's just taking advantage of you, Richard,' she told me. 'You're a tool he can use however he likes. He knows you can't refuse him.'

She was right. I knew it. I was embarrassed that my wife should see me helpless. But what could I do?

There were Irish risings against Norman power, and new battles to be fought. I fought them in the king's name as best I could, a battered old knight going out in a cause that was not really his. In time I held much of Leinster, though not as its king.

The man who might have made the best king, Donal Mac Murrough Kavanaugh, was fighting his own wars, the old story of Irish tribe against Irish tribe. Leinster was no longer a kingdom. It was just a large section of Ireland, which I held for Henry.

Henry Plantagenet was a clever man. He knew I must be given some reward, some time. In August of 1173 he appointed me 'Guardian of Ireland', a title of his own inventing.

I then awarded part of Carlow to Raymond le Gros, so my sister's husband held rich lands at last. I also made him Constable of Leinster, a title of my inventing.

My Aoife gave me strong sons, Irish sons, who were christened each in turn in the cathedral I had built, Christ Church, in Dublin.

I was more lucky in my sons than King Henry in his. His three eldest joined with the King of France against their father.

'King Henry has sent for me to fight with him in France,' I had to report to Aoife. I knew she wouldn't be pleased.

'He's only trying to get you out of Ireland because he's afraid you're becoming too strong here, Richard.'

'I know,' I said. 'But I must go. I've sworn my loyalty to him.'

'That wouldn't have stopped my father,' Aoife muttered under her breath.

With a heavy heart, I entrusted myself to the sea once more, and spent another miserable journey. But we did well once we got to France. Old as I was, I fought bravely. My only thoughts were to get back to Ireland. Even Henry had to admit that none of his barons served him better, and as a reward I was at last to go home again.

When I returned to Leinster, everyone was talking about my wife. I hurried to our stronghold at Kilkenny to learn the truth for myself.

We had built a motte and bailey of earthwork and timber, at first, but then built atop this with good stonework. As I drew near the fortress I could see signs of scorching on the stones. Someone had built a fire against the wall, trying to burn out my family.

I lashed my poor horse as hard as I could and galloped for the gates. A sentry opened them to me.

'Where is Aoife?' I cried, stepping from my horse.

She came running down the steps towards me, laughing. The sunlight caught her hair and set it ablaze. 'Here I am!' she called, holding out her hands to me. 'And here is your castle, still safe and still yours.'

The stories I had heard were true. Sitting in the great hall that night, Aoife told me everything.

'Some of O'Rourke's old army, and some of the O'Quinn tribe, besieged us while you were away,' she said. 'They called you terrible names and swore to destroy your stronghold and even your memory. Your men-at-arms defended us well, but our enemies were strong and couldn't be broken. The fighting went on and on around the walls of the castle.

'Your captain of the guard told me to stay out of sight, but at last I couldn't. I got up on a stool and took one of your swords from the wall in the armoury. Then I climbed up onto one of the outer walls, just above the heaviest fighting. The leaders of the enemy were below me. They didn't see me.

'I held your sword above my head and gave a great cry, and leaped off the wall onto them. I am so large and jumped from such a height that I broke the neck of one of them, and the rest ran away in fear. Our own men pursued them then and drove them out of the area. They haven't returned,' she added with a laugh.

I should think they hadn't! My Red Eva with a sword in her hands would be enough to put the heart crosswise in the bravest man.

After that, when I had to be away from home I didn't put the captain of the guard in charge. Aoife was in charge, and everyone knew it.

Faded Hopes

When Richard had heard my story, I took him outside and showed him the pit beyond the walls of the castle where we had buried his enemies. Together he and I put stones on their cairn. He was very proud of me.

He brought gifts for me from France, silks to wear and tapestries to hang on the walls of my chamber. I was to live like a queen, even if I wasn't one.

In my heart I was a queen. And Strongbow was King of Leinster.

The warring never ended. Knowing that Henry was kept busy with his own problems, some of the Irish princes rose against him and Richard had to fight again and again. He had learned the lessons of battle well. The Irish warriors, each fighting in his own way, were no match for our knights and ordered columns of foot soldiers. Richard held Leinster, Hugh de Lacy held Meath. In time, the old High King, Rory O'Connor, treated for peace with the King of England. With Laurence O'Toole as witness, a treaty was drawn up between them. The High King of Ireland gave his daughter to Hugh de Lacy in marriage – the same daughter who had once planned to marry my brother, Conor.

The Normans were becoming very thickly interwoven into the tapestry of Ireland, like the threads of red and blue and yellow and brown on the hangings on my walls.

Even this treaty did not stop the fighting, however.

We learned of a revolt in the west, where Irish warriors were attacking a Norman garrison established at Limerick. Richard and I were in Dublin at the time for the christening of our newest son. Raymond le Gros and his wife Basilia were with us, to stand as godparents to the boy.

'You must take a force of men to Limerick,' Richard ordered Raymond after the ceremony.

'You're not going yourself?'

'I'm tired,' Richard said. 'I'm very tired. And I have an ulcer on my foot that won't heal.'

Suddenly I was worried.

Raymond departed with a large company of men, and I put my husband to bed in the timber palace that had been built for the English king. There I watched over Richard as his strength faded, day by day. It wasn't just the ulcer on his foot. It was a total weariness of body and spirit.

I remembered how weary my father had been, at the end.

I refused to leave Richard's side. My attendants brought me food and drink, even my favourite, mushrooms with roasted hazelnuts. But I only nibbled, and sipped the French wine Richard liked. I could taste nothing.

Sometimes during those long hours my husband and I talked.

'What's happening beyond the walls of Dublin?' he wanted to know.

'We hear the usual things. The Irish are fighting the Irish, the Irish are fighting the Normans, the Normans are fighting each other.

Everyone wants to grab some piece of land, some prize someone else claims.'

Richard sighed. 'It's always like that, Aoife. I hoped …' His voice faded away.

I bent closer. 'You hoped what?'

'I hoped Ireland would be different,' he said.

He lay quietly for a long time. I held his hand and wiped his brow and watched the shadows grow longer. Pain was growing in me like a flower, waiting to bloom.

At last I knew I must send for the priest.

Leaving my husband alone with his confessor, I went outside. After the stale air of the chamber, it was good to fill my lungs with the wind off the sea and the smells coming from the smoky cooking fires in the tiny houses thronging the laneways.

I looked up. The first stars were just appearing. They swam in a sky as deep and blue as the sea Richard had crossed to come to me.

I stared at them for a while, then I went back inside.

The priest looked up as I entered the chamber and shook his head. My husband lay with his eyes closed. A rosary was threaded between his fingers.

* * *

Strongbow had changed my world so much it could never be changed back, and now he was dead.

It hurt too much to cry.

* * *

The Norman knights left after him, whom the English king had made barons, would begin quarrelling at once over his lands. I knew them well enough for that. And news of his death would encourage

152

new risings among the Irish as well. Those who had feared Strongbow would make the most of their chance.

We had to keep his death a secret from them for as long as we could, while we prepared to defend what was ours.

I thought fast. Richard would expect it of me. 'Send word to your husband to return here from Limerick with all speed,' I ordered Basilia. 'We must have Raymond's army on this side of the country, in Leinster. Send the message in code, in case it should fall into the wrong hands.'

'In code?' Basilia stared at me with wide eyes. 'But I can't even write my name!'

I lost my patience. 'I'll write it myself and sign your name for you,' I snapped at her. She nodded meekly. I think she was afraid of me.

A priest carried the message. Escorted by a picked band of my husband's most trusted men, he slipped from the gate in a covering fog and set off for Limerick. The message for Raymond read, 'Your wife Basilia desires you to know that the large molar tooth that was in so much pain has fallen out. So I beg you return quickly and without delay.'

Raymond understood. He had known Richard was unwell before he left.

As swiftly as he could, he withdrew his men from Limerick and brought them east to guard the ports and Leinster. Then he came in person to Dublin to be with us for Richard's funeral.

When we released the news of Strongbow's death, both Norman and Irish nobles came flooding into Dublin. Men in chain mail suspiciously eyed men in saffron tunics. They were as different as chalk and cheese.

Richard and I had been very different too, yet we had made a marriage. We had learned to respect and support one another. Could

Ireland make a marriage of what was left after Strongbow? I didn't know the answer.

Archbishop O'Toole, at my request, conducted my husband's funeral rites. He didn't mention the quarrel between them. He spoke only of Richard's courage and courtesy, and his Christian generosity. The barons and the princes listened gravely. Their eyes were on the long body stretched out on its funeral bier. The hands were folded over a sword that would not be used again.

Strongbow had found peace.

In the Year of Our Lord 1176, Richard de Clare was buried in a tomb in the cathedral he had built.

Every day for the rest of that sorrowful summer I wreathed his tomb with flowers.

Red Eva

Some of you may wonder what became of Aoife after Strongbow's death. She was still a young woman when her husband died, and she was to live for many years afterwards. She devoted herself to raising their sons and to defending the territory Strongbow had claimed in Ireland.

Aoife built a fortress tower at Cappamore, from which she conducted a long feud with members of Clan Quinn, who refused to grant the Normans any rights to their lands. The *Kilkenny Chronicles* describe Aoife's chambers as being hung with silk and wool, with furs spread on the couches and floors. To the end of her days, Aoife would live as an Irish princess, enjoying life and defying her enemies.

We do not know the year in which she died, but we do know how she died. Well into middle age, she was planning to leave her tower at Cappamore and was talking in the courtyard to the captain of her guards when one of the Quinns shot her through the throat – with an arrow from a strong bow.

Red Eva MacMurrough sleeps in the crypt of Kilkenny Castle now. At her feet is a red Irish deer, carved of stone.

OTHER BOOKS
FROM THE O'BRIEN PRESS

BRIAN BORU
Morgan Llywelyn

Brian Boru grew up in an Ireland torn by wars - chieftain against chieftain, tribe against tribe - and devastated by the Vikings. A fearless fighter, Brian was also a clever, educated man who learned the ways of his enemies and overcame prejudice and treachery to become High King of Ireland. This exciting, real-life story brings tenth-century Ireland vividly to life as never before.

Paperback €7.95/STG£5.99

RED HUGH
Deborah Lisson

Ireland in 1587 was a tough place. The old Irish clans struggled desperately to hold on to their lands as Queen Elizabeth I set out determinedly to subdue them. A few weeks before his fifteenth birthday, Red Hugh O'Donnell, son of the powerful O'Donnell chief of Donegal, is captured and taken to Dublin Castle. After several years, one freezing winter's night the chance of escape seems to come at last. But there are great risks ...

Paperback €6.34/STG£4.99

GRANUAILE
Morgan LLywelyn

In the sixteenth century, Granuaile, the Pirate Queen, warrior and leader, was the terror of the North Atlantic and the most feared woman in Ireland. Heading a large army and a fleet of ships, she lived by trading and raiding and demanding tribute from all who sailed through her territory. Told partly through letters written to her son Tibbot, *Granuaile* charts the gradual decline of the Gaelic chieftains and the old traditions of Ireland as Queen Elizabeth I extended her power throughout Ireland. A story of immense bravery and daring, charting the life of an incredible woman.

Paperback €6.95/STG£4.99

FARAWAY HOME
Marilyn Taylor
Winner Bisto Book of the Year Award

Two Jewish children are sent from Nazi-occupied Austria to Millisle, a refugee farm in Northern Ireland. The war has changed everything forever, and no one can tell them what their future holds. Will they ever see their families again?
Based on the true story of Millisle refugee form in Ards, County Down.

Paperback €7.95/STG£5.99

AMELIA

The year is 1914 and Amelia Pim will soon be thirteen. There are rumours of war and rebellion, and Dublin is holding its breath for major, dramatic events. But all that matters to Amelia is what she will wear to her birthday party and how she will be the envy of her friends. But where are Amelia's friends when disaster strikes her family? Now that the Pims have come down in the world, what use will Amelia have for a shimmering emerald-green dress? When Mama's political activities bring the final disgrace, it is Amelia who must hold the family together. Only the friendship of the servant girl Mary Ann seems to promise any hope.

Paperback €6.95/STG£4.99

NO PEACE FOR AMELIA

It's 1916 but Amelia Pim's thoughts are on Frederick Goodbody and not on the war in Europe. Then Frederick enlists. The pacifist Quaker community is shocked, but Amelia is secretly proud of her hero and goes to the quayside to wave him farewell. For her friend MaryAnn there are problems too, due to her brother's involvement in the Easter Rising. What will become of the two young men? And what effect will it have on the lives of Amelia and Mary Ann?

A story of conflict, hope and courage. Sequel to the No.1 bestseller Amelia.

Paperback €6.95/STG£4.99

UNDER THE HAWTHORN TREE

Winner International Reading Association Award; Reading Association of Ireland Award

Ireland in the 1840s is devastated by famine. When tragedy strikes their family, Eily, Michael and Peggy are left to fend for themselves. Starving and in danger of ending up in the dreaded workhouse, they escape. Their one hope is to find the great-aunts they have heard about in their mother's stories.

Paperback €7.95/STG£5.99

Send for our full-colour catalogue

ORDER FORM

Please send me the books as marked.

I enclose cheque/postal order for € . . . .

(Please include €2.50 P&P per title)

OR please charge my credit card ☐ Access/Mastercard ☐ Visa

Card Number __ __ __ __   __ __ __ __   __ __ __ __   __ __ __ __

Expiry Date __ __ / __ __

Name. . . . . Tel . . . .

Address . . . .

. . . .

Please send orders to: THE O'BRIEN PRESS, 20 Victoria Road, Dublin 6, Ireland.

Tel: +353 1 4923333; Fax: +353 1 4922777; E-mail: books@obrien.ie

Website: www.obrien.ie

Please note: prices are subject to change without notice